MY LIFE WITH
SHERLOCK HOLMES

Upper Baker Street, circa 1905
(*City of Westminster Libraries, Archives Department*)

Baker Street and Portman Museum, circa 1900
(*City of Westminster Libraries, Archives Department*)

MY LIFE WITH
SHERLOCK HOLMES

—

*Conversations in Baker Street
by John H. Watson, M.D.*

—

EDITED BY J. R. HAMILTON

HAWTHORN BOOKS, INC.
Publishers / New York

First published in the United States in 1976.

CONTENTS

CONTENTS

MY LIFE WITH
SHERLOCK HOLMES

ACKNOWLEDGMENTS

Grateful thanks to Mr. Adrian Conan Doyle and the Trustees of the Sir Arthur Conan Doyle Estate for kind permission to use this selection from his father's books, and to Miss Jane Boulenger and my son Dr. Gervase Hamilton for reading the typescript and making some useful suggestions. Also to my son for assisting me in the task of proof-reading.

J.R.H.

EDITOR'S FOREWORD

Most people have heard of Sherlock Holmes and Dr. Watson, but there are many, especially among the young, who have not read the Sherlock Holmes stories, and for them this book may serve as an introduction. It presents a close-up portrait of Holmes – his appearance and outlook, his temperament, character and intellect – as seen and recorded by his friend Dr. Watson through their day to day life and conversations in the room they shared at 22 1B Baker Street.

Sherlock Holmes believed in method, and following his example, the editor would like to explain his own method in arranging and selecting these conversations. The first thing was to find a form and sequence for the material: to build it up into a series of logically related chapters, each covering some aspect of Holmes. Next came the problem of selection. In order to produce a continuous narrative from what are often brief scraps of conversation scattered throughout two long volumes, some pruning was inevitable. But all essential aspects of Sherlock Holmes have been preserved. Not everything in this book was spoken by Holmes in the Baker Street room: he repeated himself quite often in different places and contexts, and in the course of his conversations with Watson he often returned to subjects they had discussed outside. Lastly came the problem of continuity and the time factor. It was essential to introduce a few editorial interpolations as links, and occasionally to make a resumé of Watson's words. It is hoped that Sherlockian scholars will not object to this editorial intervention in the cause of continuity.

Apart from the brief introductory chapter, the entire book is set in the living-room in Baker Street. No third party is introduced: other characters emerge only from the conversation. The two friends are alone – except for the reader, who is now invited, a silent and unseen guest, to enter the famous room.

Sherlock Holmes's sitting-room at 221B Baker Street (City of Westminster Libraries, Archives Department)

OUR FIRST MEETING

'Dr. Watson, Mr. Sherlock Holmes,' said Stamford, introducing us.

'How are you?' he said cordially, gripping my hand with a strength for which I should hardly have given him credit.

'My friend here wants to take diggings,' said Stamford; 'and as you were complaining that you could get no one to go halves with you, I thought that I had better bring you together.'

Sherlock Holmes seemed delighted at the idea of sharing his rooms with me. 'I have my eye on a suite in Baker Street,' he said, 'which would suit us down to the ground. You don't mind the smell of strong tobacco, I hope?'

'I always smoke "ship's" myself,' I answered.

'That's good enough. I generally have chemicals about, and occasionally do experiments. Would that annoy you?'

'By no means.'

'Let me see – what are my other shortcomings. I get in the dumps at times, and don't open my mouth for days on end. You must not think I am sulky when I do that. Just let me alone, and I'll soon be right. What have you to confess now? It's just as well for two fellows to know the worst of one another before they begin to live together.'

I laughed at this cross-examination. 'I object to row, because my nerves are shaken, and I get up at all sorts of ungodly hours, and I am extremely lazy.'

'Do you include violin playing in your category of rows?' he asked anxiously.

'It depends on the player,' I answered. 'A well-played violin is a treat for the gods – a badly-played one —'

'Oh, that's all right,' he cried with a merry laugh. 'I think we may consider the thing as settled – that is if the rooms are agreeable to you.'

'When shall we see them?'

'Call for me here at noon tomorrow, and we'll go together and settle everything,' he answered.

*   *   *   *

We met next day as he had arranged, and inspected the rooms at 221B Baker Street. They consisted of a couple of comfortable bedrooms and a single large airy sitting-room, cheerfully furnished, and illuminated by two broad windows. So desirable in every way were the apartments, and so moderate did the terms seem when divided between us, that the bargain was concluded upon the spot, and we at once entered into possession. That very evening I moved my things round from the hotel, and on the following morning Sherlock Holmes followed me with several boxes and portmanteaus. For a day or two we were busily employed in unpacking and laying out our property to the best advantage. That done, we gradually began to settle down and to accommodate ourselves to our new surroundings.

City of London street, circa 1900
(*Mansell Collection*)

THE MAN HOLMES

It was a bright, crisp February morning, and the snow of the day before still lay deep upon the ground, shimmering brightly in the wintry sun. Down the centre of Baker Street it had been ploughed into a brown crumbly band by the traffic, but at either side and on the heaped-up edges of the footpaths it lay still as white as when it fell.

Sherlock Holmes, deep in thought and shrouded in a cloud of tobacco smoke, sat opposite to me on the other side of our cheerful fire. His person and appearance were such as to strike the attention of the most casual observer. In height he was rather over six feet, and so excessively lean that he seemed to be considerably taller. His eyes were sharp and piercing, save during intervals of torpor; and his thin hawk-like nose gave his whole expression an air of alertness and decision. His chin, too, had the prominence and squareness which mark the man of determination. His hands were invariably blotted with ink and stained with chemicals, yet he was possessed of extraordinary delicacy of touch. His voice was high and somewhat strident. Sometimes he had a pleased and yet critical face, like a connoisseur who had just taken his first sip of a comet vintage. He also had, when he so willed it, the utter immobility of countenance of a Red Indian. There were times when his head was sunk upon his breast, and he looked from my point of view like a strange, lank bird, with dull grey plumage and a black top-knot.

*   *   *   *

I was impressed by the discretion and high sense of professional honour which distinguished my friend.

'I think I may go so far as to say, Watson, that I have not lived wholly in vain,' he remarked. 'If my record were closed I could still survey it with equanimity. The air of London is the sweeter for my presence.'

More than once I had observed that a small vanity underlay my companion's quiet and didactic manner. It was one of the peculiarities of his proud, self-contained nature that, though he docketed any fresh information very quickly and accurately in his brain, he seldom made any acknowledgement to the giver.

'You have brought detection as near an exact science as it ever will be brought in this world.'

My companion flushed up with pleasure at my words, and the earnest way in which I uttered them. I had already observed that he was as sensitive to flattery on the score of his art as any girl could be of her beauty. At the same time to his sombre and cynical spirit all popular applause was always abhorrent, and nothing amused him more at the end of a successful case than to hand over the actual exposure to some orthodox official, and to listen with a mocking smile to the general chorus of misplaced congratulation.

Holmes, like all great artists, lived for his art's sake. So unworldly was he – or so capricious – that he frequently refused his help to the powerful and wealthy where the problem made no appeal to his sympathies, while he would devote weeks of most intense application to the affairs of some humble client whose case presented those strange and dramatic qualities which appealed to his imagination and challenged his ingenuity.

'I have chosen my own particular profession, or rather created it, for I am the only one in the world.'

'The only unofficial detective?' I said, raising my eyebrows.

'The only unofficial consulting detective,' he answered. 'I am the last and highest court of appeal in detection. When Gregson, or Lestrade, or Athelney Jones are out of their depths – which, by the way, is their normal state – the matter is laid before me. I examine the data, as an expert, and pronounce a specialist's opinion. I claim no credit in such cases. My name figures in no newspaper. The work itself, the pleasure of finding a field for my peculiar powers, is my highest reward.'

*　　*　　*　　*

Holmes was not a difficult man to live with. He was quiet in his ways, and his habits were regular. It was rare for him to be up after ten at night, and he had often breakfasted and gone out before I rose in the morning. Sometimes he spent his day at the chemical laboratory, sometimes in the dissecting rooms, and occasionally in long walks, which appeared to take him into the lowest portions of the city.

Nothing could exceed his energy when the working fit was upon him; but now and again a reaction would seize him, and for days on end he would lie upon the sofa in the sitting-room, hardly uttering a word or moving a muscle from morning to night. That razor brain blunted and rusted with inaction. Sherlock Holmes's eyes glistened, his pale cheeks took a warmer hue, and his whole eager face shone with an inward light when the call for work reached him. He had the impersonal joy of the true artist in his better work, even as he mourned darkly when it fell below the high level to which he aspired.

He could talk exceedingly well when he chose and often spoke on a quick succession of subjects – on miracle plays, on medieval pottery, on Stradivarius violins, on the Buddhism of Ceylon, and on warships of the future – handling each as though he had made a special study of it. His bright humour marked the reaction from black depression.

* * * *

One wild morning in October – I observed as I was dressing how the last remaining leaves were being whirled from the solitary plane tree which graces the yard behind our house – I descended to breakfast prepared to find my companion in depressed spirits, for, like all great artists he was easily impressed by his surroundings. On the contrary, I found that he had nearly finished his meal, and that his mood was particularly bright and joyous, with that somewhat sinister cheerfulness which was characteristic of his lighter moments.

'You have a case, Holmes?' I remarked.

'The faculty of deduction is certainly contagious, Watson,' he answered. 'It has enabled you to probe my secret. Yes, I have a case.'

'Might I share it?'

'There is little to share, but we may discuss it when you have consumed the two hard-boiled eggs with which our

cook has favoured us. Their condition may not be uncon-
nected with the copy of the *Family Herald* which I observed
yesterday upon the hall-table. Even so trivial a matter as
cooking an egg demands an attention which is conscious
of the passage of time, and incompatible with the love
romance in that excellent periodical.'

All that day and the next and the next Holmes was in a
mood which his friends would call taciturn, and others
morose. He ran out and ran in, smoked incessantly,
played snatches on his violin, sank into reveries, devoured
sandwiches at irregular hours, and hardly answered the
casual questions which I put to him. Sometimes he would
bite his nails and stare blankly out of the window. At
other times he was tense and alert, his eyes shining, his
face set, his limbs quivering with eager activity.

Sometimes he would act on sudden impulses. One bitterly cold and frosty morning I was wakened by a tugging at
my shoulder. It was Holmes. The candle in his hand shone
upon his eager, stooping face. 'Come, Watson, come!' he
cried. 'The game is afoot. Not a word! Into your clothes
and come!'

* * * *

An anomaly which often struck me in my friend's
character was that, although in his methods of thought he
was the neatest and most methodical of mankind, and
although also he affected a certain quiet primness of dress,
he was none the less in his personal habits one of the most
untidy men that ever drove a fellow-lodger to distraction.
Not that I am in the least conventional in that respect

myself. The rough-and-tumble work in Afghanistan, coming on the top of a natural Bohemianism of disposition, has made me rather more lax than befits a medical man. But with me there is a limit, and when I find a man who keeps his cigars in the coal-scuttle, his tobacco in the toe-end of a Persian slipper, and his unanswered correspondence transfixed by a jack-knife into the very centre of his wooden mantelpiece, then I begin to give myself virtuous airs. I have always held, too, that pistol practice should distinctly be an open-air pastime; and when Holmes in one of his queer humours would sit in an arm-chair, with his hair-trigger and a hundred Boxer cartridges, and proceed to adorn the opposite wall with a patriotic V.R. done in bullet-pocks, I felt strongly that neither the atmosphere nor the appearance of our room was improved by it.

Our chambers were always full of chemicals and of criminal relics, which had a way of wandering into unlikely positions, and of turning up in the butter-dish or even in less desirable places. But his papers were my great crux. He had a horror of destroying documents, especially those which were connected with his past cases, and yet it was only once in every year or two that he would muster energy to docket and arrange them, for as I have said, the outbursts of passionate energy when he performed the remarkable feats with which his name is associated were followed by reactions of lethargy, during which he would lie about with his violin and his books, hardly moving, save from the sofa to the table. Thus month after month his papers accumulated, until every corner of the room was stacked with bundles of manuscript which were

on no account to be burned, and which could not be put
away save by their owner.

*　　*　　*　　*

One winter's night, as we sat together by the fire, I
ventured to suggest to him that as he had finished pasting
extracts into his commonplace book he might employ the
next two hours in making our room a little more habitable.
He could not deny the justice of my request, so with a
rather rueful face he went off to his bedroom, from which
he returned presently pulling a large tin box behind
him. This he placed in the middle of the floor, and
squatting down upon a stool in front of it he threw back
the lid. I could see that it was already a third full of
bundles of paper tied up with red tape into separate
packages.

'There are cases enough here, Watson,' said he, looking
at me with mischievous eyes, 'I think that if you knew all
that I have put in this box you would ask me to pull some
out instead of putting others in.'

'These are the records of your early work, then?' I
asked. 'I have often wished I had notes of those cases.'

'Yes, my boy; these were all done prematurely, before
my biographer had come to glorify me.' He lifted bundle
after bundle in a tender, caressing sort of way. 'They are
not all successes, Watson,' said he, 'but there are some
pretty little problems among them. Here's the record of
the Tarleton murders, and the case of Vamberry, the
wine merchant, and the adventure of the old Russian
woman, and the singular affair of the aluminium crutch,

as well as a full account of Ricoletti of the club foot and his abominable wife.'

I had often endeavoured to elicit from my companion what had first turned his mind in the direction of criminal research, but I had never caught him before in such a communicative humour. Now he sat forward in his arm-chair, and spread out the documents upon his knees. Then he lit his pipe and sat for some time smoking and turning them over.

'Burglary,' he said, 'has always been an alternative profession, had I cared to adopt it, and I have little doubt that I should have come to the front.'

*   *   *   *

Holmes confessed to me that he was never sociable, and only made one friend during the two years he was at college. 'I was never a very sociable fellow, Watson, always rather fond of moping in my rooms and working out my own little methods of thought, so that I never mixed much with the men of my year.' Sometimes after a case he looked utterly weary. 'I shall be limp as a rag for a week.' 'Strange,' said I, 'how terms of what in another man I should call laziness alternate with your fits of splendid energy and vigour.' 'Yes,' he answered, 'there are the makings in me of a very fine loafer, and also of a pretty spry sort of fellow.'

He was often late in the mornings, save on those not infrequent occasions when he stayed up all night. Then, when I came down to breakfast, I would find him pale and harassed, his bright eyes the brighter for the dark shadows round them. He would have no breakfast himself, for it was one of his peculiarities that in his more intense moments he would permit himself no food. 'At present I cannot spare energy and nerve force for digestion,' he would say in answer to my medical remonstrances.

It was no uncommon thing for him to be away for days and nights on end when he was hot upon a scent.

* * * *

Holmes hated boredom. 'You reasoned it out beautifully,' I exclaimed at the end of a case. 'It is a long chain, and yet every link rings true.' 'It saved me from ennui,' he answered, yawning. 'Alas, I already feel it closing in upon me! My life is spent in one long effort to escape from the commonplaces of existence. These little problems help me to do so. My mind is like a racing engine, tearing itself to pieces because it is not connected up with the work for which it was built.'

In the spring of 1897 Holmes's iron constitution showed some symptoms of giving way, and Dr. Moore Agar, of Harley Street, whose dramatic introduction to Holmes I may some day recount, gave positive injunctions that the famous private agent would lay aside all his cases and surrender himself to complete rest if he wished to avert an absolute breakdown. The state of his health was not a matter in which he himself took the faintest interest, for his mental detachment was absolute, but he was induced at last, on the threat of being permanently disqualified from work, to give himself a complete change of scene and air.

* * * *

Sherlock Holmes was a man who when he had an unsolved problem upon his mind would go for days, and even for a week, without rest, turning it over, rearranging his facts, looking at it from every point of view, until he had either fathomed it, or convinced himself that his data was insufficient. There was something ice-cold in his reasoning. Yet he did not appear to have pursued any course of reading which might fit him for a degree in science or any other recognized portal which would give him an entrance into the learned world.

His zeal for certain studies was remarkable, and within eccentric limits his knowledge was so extraordinarily ample and minute that his observations have fairly astounded me. Surely no man would work so hard or attain such precise information unless he had some definite end in view. Desultory readers are seldom remarkable for the exactness of their learning. No man burdens his mind with small matters unless he has some very good reason for doing so.

His ignorance was as remarkable as his knowledge. Of contemporary literature, philosophy and politics he appeared to know next to nothing.

'You see,' he explained, 'I consider that a man's brain originally is like a little empty attic, and you have to stock it with such furniture as you choose. A fool takes in all the lumber of every sort that he comes across, so that the knowledge which might be useful to him gets crowded out, or at best is jumbled up with a lot of other things, so that he has a difficulty in laying his hands upon it. Now the skilled workman is very careful indeed as to what he takes into his brain-attic. He will have nothing but the tools which may help him in doing his work, but of these he has a large assortment, and all in the most perfect order. It is a mistake to think that the little room has elastic walls and can distend to any extent. Depend upon it there comes a time when for every addition of knowledge you forget something which you knew before. It is of the highest importance, therefore, not to have useless facts elbowing out the useful ones.'

He said that he would acquire no knowledge which did not bear upon his object.* Therefore all the knowledge which he possessed was such as would be useful to him. I enumerated in my own mind all the various points upon which he had shown me that he was exceptionally well-informed. I even took a pencil and jotted them down. I could not help smiling at the document when I had completed it. It ran in this way:

Knowledge of literature, philosophy and astronomy, nil: politics, feeble: botany, variable – well up in belladonna, opium, and poisons generally: geology, practical but limited – tells at a glance different soils from each other, and after walks has shown me splashes upon his trousers, and told me by their colour and consistence in what part of London he had received them. Knowledge of chemistry profound: of anatomy, accurate but unsystematic. Knowledge of sensational literature, immense – he appears to know every detail of every horror perpetrated in the century.

* In the course of this conversation Holmes said that he was ignorant of the Copernican Theory, e.g. that the earth travelled round the sun. He was obviously pulling Watson's leg. But Watson must have been very obtuse to have believed him. The episode is best forgotten – EDITOR.

When I had got so far on my list I threw it on the fire in despair.

Fortunately I kept most of my other notes. In glancing over the notes of cases in which I had studied the methods of my friend, I find many tragic, some comic, a large number merely strange, but none commonplace; for, working as he did rather for the love of his art than for the acquirement of wealth, he refused to associate himself with any investigation which did not tend towards the unusual, and even the fantastic.

Marleybone Road, 1900
(*City of Westminster Libraries, Archives Department*)

Paddington Station, 1896
(*City of Westminster Libraries, Archives Department*)

HIS INTERESTS AND TASTES

It was a bitterly cold morning during the winter of '97. I seated myself in my arm-chair, and warmed my hands before the crackling fire, for a sharp frost had set in, and the windows were thick with ice crystals. Holmes was seated at his side-table clad in his dressing-gown and working hard over a chemical investigation. A large curved retort was boiling furiously in the bluish flame of a Bunsen burner, and the distilled drops were condensing into a two-litre measure. He dipped into this bottle or that, drawing out a few drops of each with his glass pipette, and finally brought a test-tube containing a solution over to the table. In his right hand he had a slip of litmus-paper.

'We are at a crisis, Watson,' said he. 'If this paper remains blue, all is well. If it turns red, it means a man's life.' He dipped it into the test-tube, and it flushed at once into a dull dirty crimson.

'Hum! I thought as much!' he cried. 'I shall be at your service in one instant, Watson. You will find tobacco in the Persian slipper.' He turned to his desk and scribbled off several telegrams, then he threw himself down in the chair opposite and drew up his knees until his fingers clasped round his long, thin shins.

'A very commonplace little murder,' said he. 'You've got something better, I fancy. You are the stormy petrel of crime, Watson.'

On another occasion I found him half asleep, with his long, thin form curled up in the recesses of his arm-chair.

A formidable array of bottles and test-tubes, with the pungent cleanly smell of hydrochloric acid, told me that he had spent his day in the chemical work which was so dear to him.

'Well, have you solved it?' I asked as I entered.

'Yes. It was the bisulphate of baryta.'

'No, no, the mystery!' I cried.

'Oh, that! I thought of the salt that I have been working upon.'

*   *   *   *

Holmes sometimes dabbled in botany. 'With a spud, a tin box, and an elementary book on botany, there are instructive days to be spent.' In later years he took up bee-keeping and wrote a *Practical Handbook of Bee Culture, with some Observations upon the Segregation of the Queen* – 'the fruit of pensive nights and laborious days'. The microscope was a perennial interest. I remember him bending for a long time over a low-power microscope, then straightening himself up and looking at me in triumph.

'It is glue, Watson,' said he. 'Unquestionably it is glue. Have a look at these scattered objects in the field!'

I stooped to the eyepiece and focused for my vision.

'Those hairs are threads from a tweed coat. The irregular grey masses are dust. There are epithelial scales on the left. Those brown blobs in the centre are undoubtedly glue.'

'Well,' I said laughing, 'I am prepared to take your word for it. Does anything depend upon it?'

'It is a very fine demonstration,' he answered. 'In the

St. Pancras case you may remember that a cap was found beside the dead policeman. The accused man denies that it is his. But he is a picture-frame maker who habitually handles glue.'

'Is it one of your cases?'

'No; my friend Merivale of the Yard, asked me to look into the case. Since I ran down that coiner by the zinc and copper filings in the seam of his cuff they have begun to realize the importance of the microscope.'

*   *   *   *

'I have a box for *Les Huguenots*. Have you heard the De Reszkes?'* Holmes's love of music extended to the opera and concert hall. One evening after a concert he was late in returning, and dinner was on the table before he appeared.

'It was magnificent,' he said, as he took his seat. 'Do you remember what Darwin says about music? He claims that the power of producing and appreciating it existed among the human race long before the power of speech was arrived at. Perhaps that is why we are so subtly influenced by it. There are vague memories in our souls of those misty centuries when the world was in its childhood.'

'That's rather a broad idea,' I remarked.

'One's ideas must be as broad as Nature if they are to interpret Nature,' he answered.

*   *   *   *

---

* Opera by Meyerbeer with Jean and Edouard De Reszke, the tenor and baritone, the singers then at the height of their fame.

Holmes's powers on the violin were very remarkable, but as eccentric as all his other accomplishments. That he could play pieces, and difficult pieces, I knew well, because at my request he has played me some of Mendelssohn's Lieder, and other favourites. When left to himself, however, he would seldom produce any music or attempt any recognized air. Leaning back in his arm-chair of an evening, he would close his eyes and scrape carelessly at the fiddle which was thrown across his knee.*

I remember him returning from a case late one evening and I could see by a glance at his haggard and anxious face that the high hopes with which he started had not been fulfilled. For an hour he droned away upon his violin, endeavouring to soothe his own ruffled spirits.

Sometimes the sounds made by Holmes were sonorous and melancholy. Occasionally they were fantastic and cheerful. Clearly they reflected the thoughts which possessed him, but whether the music aided those thoughts, or whether the playing was simply the result of a whim or fancy, was more than I could determine.

I might have rebelled against these exasperating solos had it not been that he usually terminated them by playing in quick succession a whole series of my favourite airs as a slight compensation for the trial upon my patience.

During one memorable meal, Holmes would talk about nothing but violins, narrating with great exultation how he had purchased his own Stradivarius, which was worth at least five hundred guineas, at a Jew broker's in Tottenham Court Road for fifty-five shillings. This led him to

* Across his knee? One would like to know more about this unusual method of violin playing – EDITOR.

Paganini, and we sat for an hour over a bottle of claret while he told me anecdote after anecdote of that extraordinary man.

*　　*　　*　　*

One of the most remarkable characteristics of Sherlock Holmes was his power of throwing his brain out of action and switching all his thoughts on to lighter things whenever he had convinced himself that he could no longer work to advantage. I remember that during a whole day he lost himself in a monograph which he had undertaken upon the Polyphonic Motets of Lassus. It has since been printed for private circulation, and is said by experts to be the last word upon the subject.

*　　*　　*　　*

Sherlock Holmes was a man who seldom took exercise for exercise's sake. Few men were capable of greater muscular effort, and he was undoubtedly one of the finest boxers of his weight that I have ever seen; but he looked upon aimless bodily exertion as a waste of energy, and he seldom bestirred himself save where there was some professional object to be served. But he once said to me, 'There can be no question, my dear Watson, of the value of exercise before breakfast.'

*　　*　　*　　*

Holmes was a great smoker and found tobacco an aid to thought. I remember asking him what he was going to do about some difficult problem.

'To smoke,' he answered. 'It is quite a three-pipe problem, and I beg that you won't speak to me for fifty minutes.' He curled himself up in his chair, with his thin knees drawn up to his hawk-like nose, and there he sat with his eyes closed and his black clay pipe thrusting out like the bill of some strange bird.

Sometimes in the morning I would find him lounging about in his dressing-gown, reading the agony column of *The Times*, and smoking his before-breakfast pipe, which was composed of all the plugs and dottles left from his smokes of the day before, all carefully dried and collected on the corner of the mantelpiece.*

I have known him to sit silent with his finger-tips pressed together, his legs stretched out in front of him, and his gaze directed upwards to the ceiling. Then he would take down from the rack the old and oily clay pipe, which was to him as a counsellor, and, having lit it, lean back in his chair, with the thick blue cloud-wreaths spinning up from him, and a look of infinite languor in his face. I have seen him sit in silence with his head sunk forward, and his eyes bent upon the red glow of the fire, then light his pipe, and leaning back in his chair watch the blue smoke rings as they chased each other up to the ceiling. I have watched him coiled in his arm-chair, his haggard and ascetic face hardly visible amid the blue swirl of his tobacco smoke, his black brows drawn down, his forehead contracted, his eyes vacant and far away.

I recall arriving back from my club one evening at about

* He must have been very hard up at the time, considering that quite good tobacco was about 6d. an ounce – EDITOR.

nine o'clock and my first impression as I opened the door was that a fire had broken out, for the room was so filled with smoke that the light of the lamp upon the table was blurred by it. As I entered, however, my fears were set at rest, for it was the acrid fumes of strong, coarse tobacco, which took me by the throat and set me coughing. Through the haze I had a vision of Holmes in his dressing-gown coiled up in an arm-chair with his black clay pipe between his lips. Several rolls of paper lay around him.

'Caught cold, Watson?' said he.

'No, it's this poisonous atmosphere.'

'I suppose it *is* pretty thick, now that you mention it.'

'Thick! It is intolerable.'

'Open the window, then!'

How often have I left him smoking hard, with his heavy, dark brows knotted together, and his long nervous fingers tapping upon the arms of his chair, as he turned over in his mind every possible solution of a mystery.

* * * *

But, alas, tobacco was not the only stimulant to which my friend was addicted. I remember my feeling of shock the first time I saw him take a bottle from the corner of the mantelpiece and a hypodermic syringe from its neat morocco case. With his long, white, nervous fingers he adjusted the delicate needle, and rolled back his left shirt-cuff. For some little time his eyes rested thoughtfully upon the sinewy forearm and wrist, all dotted and scarred with innumerable puncture-marks. Finally, he thrust the sharp point home, pressed down the tiny piston, and sank back into the velvet-lined arm-chair with a long sigh of satisfaction.

Three times a day for many months I had witnessed this performance, but custom had not reconciled my mind to it. On the contrary, from day to day I had become more irritable at the sight, and my conscience swelled nightly within me at the thought that I had lacked the courage to protest.* Again and again I had registered a vow that I should deliver my soul upon the subject; but there was that in the cool, nonchalant air of my companion which made him the last man with whom one would care to take anything approaching a liberty. His great powers, his masterly manner, and the experience which I had had of his many extraordinary qualities, all made me diffident and backward in crossing him.

But one afternoon, whether it was the Beaune which I had taken with my lunch, or the additional exasperation produced by the extreme deliberation of his manner, I suddenly felt that I could hold out no longer.

'Which is it today,' I asked, 'morphine or cocaine?'

He raised his eyes languidly from the old black-letter volume which he had opened.

'It is cocaine,' he said, 'a seven-per-cent solution. Would you care to try it?'

'No, indeed,' I answered brusquely. 'My constitution

* Holmes suffered from intermittent depression and took drugs as a relief. It is often forgotten that in those days there was no law against drugs, and it was not at all unusual for the old of the poorer classes to relieve their pains with cheap opium. A Derbyshire chemist recalled how he kept a lump of the sticky stuff on his counter and rheumaticky old souls would take a few pennyworth quite frequently. Watson was right in his condemnation; but we must consider the circumstances – EDITOR.

has not got over the Afghan campaign yet. I cannot afford to throw any extra strain upon it.'

He smiled at my vehemence. 'Perhaps you are right, Watson,' he said. 'I suppose that its influence is physically a bad one. I find it, however, so transcendently stimulating and clarifying to the mind that its secondary action is a matter of small moment.'

'But consider!' I said earnestly. 'Count the cost! Your brain may, as you say, be roused and excited, but it is a pathological and morbid process, which involves increased tissue-change, and may at last leave a permanent weakness. You know, too, what a black reaction comes upon you. Surely the game is hardly worth the candle. Why should you, for a mere passing pleasure, risk the loss of those great powers with which you have been endowed? Remember that I speak not only as one comrade to another, but as a medical man to one for whose constitution he is to some extent answerable.'

He did not seem offended. On the contrary, he put his finger-tips together, and leaned his elbows on the arms of his chair, like one who has a relish for conversation.

'My mind,' he said, 'rebels at stagnation. Give me problems, give me work, give me the most abstruse cryptogram, or the most intricate analysis, and I am in my own proper atmosphere. I can dispense then with artificial stimulants. But I abhor the dull routine of existence. I crave for mental exaltation.'

Gradually I weaned him from that drug mania which threatened to check his remarkable career until I knew that under ordinary conditions he would no longer crave for this artificial stimulus; but I was well aware that the fiend was not dead, but sleeping; and I have known that the sleep was a light one and the waking near when in periods of idleness I have seen the drawn look upon Holmes's ascetic face, and the brooding of his deep-set and inscrutable eyes.

*   *   *   *

Holmes's appetite for food varied with his state of mind. I have seen him with his mouth full of toast and his eyes sparkling with mischief, watching my intellectual entanglement with some problem. The mere sight of his excellent appetite was an assurance of success, for I had very clear recollections of days and nights without a thought of food, when his baffled mind had chafed before some problem whilst his thin, eager features became more attenuated with the asceticism of complete mental concentration. I have known him presume upon his iron strength until he had fainted from pure inanition. I have seen him walk to the sideboard, and, tearing a piece from the loaf, devour it voraciously, washing it down with a long draught of water.

'I am starving. I have had nothing since breakfast.'

'Nothing?'

'Not a bite. I had no time to think of it.'

But in another mood:

'There is a cold partridge on the sideboard, Watson, and a bottle of Montrachet. Let us renew our energies before we make a fresh call upon them.'

Carlisle Street, N. W. 1, with some "Baker Street Irregulars
(*City of Westminster Libraries, Archives Department*)

THE DETECTIVE

It was in the latter days of September, and the equinoctical gales had set in with exceptional violence. All day the wind had screamed and the rain had beaten against the windows, so that even here in the heart of great, handmade London we were forced to raise our minds for the instant from the routine of life, and to recognize the presence of those great elemental forces which shriek at mankind through the bars of his civilization, like untamed beasts in a cage. It was strange there in the very depths of the town, with ten miles of man's handiwork on either side of us, to feel the iron grip of Nature, and to be conscious that to the huge elemental forces, all London was no more than the molehills that dot the fields. As evening drew in the storm grew louder and louder, and the wind cried and sobbed like a child in the chimney. Outside, the wind howled down Baker Street, while the rain beat fiercely against the windows. Sherlock Holmes sat moodily on one side of the fireplace cross-indexing his records of crime, while I at the other was deep in one of Clark Russell's fine sea stories, until the howl of the gale without seemed to blend with the text, and the splash of the rain to lengthen out into the long swash of the sea waves. I walked to the window and looked out on the deserted street. The occasional lamps gleamed on the expanse of muddy road and shining pavement. A single cab was splashing its way from the Oxford Street end.

*   *   *   *

Next day I rose somewhat earlier than usual and found that Sherlock Holmes had not yet finished his breakfast. Our landlady, Mrs. Hudson, had become so accustomed to my late habits that my place had not been laid nor my coffee prepared. With the unreasonable petulance of mankind I rang the bell. Then I picked up a magazine from the table and attempted to while away the time with it, while my companion munched silently at his toast. One of the articles had a pencil mark at the heading, and I naturally began to run my eye through it.

Its somewhat ambitious title was *The Book of Life*, and it attempted to show how much an observant man might learn by an accurate and systematic examination of all that came in his way. It struck me as being a remarkable mixture of shrewdness and of absurdity. The reasoning was close and intense, but the deductions appeared to me to be far-fetched and exaggerated. The writer claimed by a momentary expression, a twitch of a muscle or a glance of an eye, to fathom a man's inmost thoughts. Deceit, according to him, was an impossibility in the case of one trained to observation and analysis. His conclusions were as infallible as so many propositions of Euclid. So startling would his results appear to the uninitiated that until they learned the processes by which he had arrived at them they might well consider him a necromancer.

From a drop of water (said the writer) a logician could infer the possibility of the Atlantic Ocean or Niagara without having seen or heard of one or the other. So all life is a great chain, the nature of which is known whenever we are shown a single link of it. Like all other arts, the Science of Deduction and Analysis is one which can only be acquired by long and patient study, nor is life long enough to allow any mortal to attain the highest possible perfection in it. Before turning to those moral and mental aspects of the matter which present the greatest difficulties, let the inquirer begin by mastering more elementary problems. Let him on meeting a fellow-mortal, learn at a glance to distinguish the history of the man, and the trade or profession to which he belongs. Puerile as such an exercise may seem, it sharpens the faculties of observation, and teaches one where to look and what to look for. By a man's finger-nails, by his coat-sleeve, by his boot, by his trouser-knees, by the callosities of his forefinger and thumb, by his expression, by his shirt-cuffs – by each of these things a man's calling is plainly revealed. That all united should fail to enlighten the competent inquirer in any case is inconceivable.

'What ineffable twaddle!' I cried, slapping the magazine down on the table.

'What is it?' asked Sherlock Holmes.

'Why, this article,' I said, pointing at it with my egg-spoon as I sat down to my breakfast. 'I see that you have read it since you have marked it. I don't deny that it is smartly written. It irritates me though. It is evidently the theory of some arm-chair lounger who evolves all these neat little paradoxes in the seclusion of his own study. It is not practical. I should like to see him clapped down in a third-class carriage on the Underground, and asked to give the trades of all his fellow-travellers. I would lay a thousand to one against him.'

'You would lose your money,' Holmes remarked calmly. 'As for the article, I wrote it myself.'

'You!'

'Yes. The theories which I have expressed there, and which appear to you so chimerical, are really extremely practical.'

'You remind me of Edgar Allen Poe's Dupin,' I said smiling. 'I had no idea that such individuals did exist outside of stories.'

Sherlock Holmes rose and lit his pipe. 'No doubt you think that you are complimenting me in comparing me to Dupin,' he observed. 'Now, in my opinion, Dupin was a very inferior fellow. That trick of his of breaking in on his friends' thoughts with an apropos remark after a quarter of an hour's silence is really very showy and superficial. He had some analytical genius, no doubt; but he was by no means such a phenomenon as Poe appears to imagine.'

'Have you read Gaboriau's works?' I asked. 'Does Lecoq come up to your idea of a detective?'

Sherlock Holmes sniffed sardonically. 'Lecoq was a miserable bungler,' he said, in an angry voice; 'he had only one thing to recommend him, and that was his energy. That book made me positively ill. The question was how to identify an unknown prisoner. I could have done it in twenty-four hours. Lecoq took six months or so. It might be made a text-book for detectives to teach them what to avoid.'

Holmes re-filled his pipe. 'I was consulted last week by François le Villard, who, as you probably know, has come rather to the front lately in the French detective service. He has all the Celtic power of quick intuition, but he is deficient in the wide range of exact knowledge which is essential to the higher developments of his art. The case was concerned with a will, and possessed some features of interest. I was able to refer him to two parallel cases which have suggested to him the true solution. Here is the letter which I had this morning acknowledging my assistance.'

He tossed over, as he spoke, a crumpled sheet of foreign notepaper. I glanced my eyes down it, catching a profusion of notes of admiration, with stray '*magnifiques*', '*coup-de-maîtres*', and '*tours-de-force*', all testifying to the ardent admiration of the Frenchman.

'He speaks as a pupil to a master,' said I.

'Oh, he rates my assistance too highly,' said Sherlock Holmes, lightly. 'He has considerable gifts himself. He possesses two out of the three qualities necessary for the ideal detective. He has the power of observation and that of deduction. He is only wanting in knowledge, and that may come in time. He is now translating my small works into French.'

*　　*　　*　　*

It was a foggy, cloudy morning, and a dun-coloured veil hung over the house-tops, looking like the reflection of the mud-coloured streets beneath. My companion was in the best of spirits, and prattled away about Cremona fiddles, and the difference between a Stradivarius and an Amati. As for myself, I was silent, for the dull weather depressed my spirits.

'You don't seem to give much thought to the matter in hand,' I said at last, interrupting Holmes's musical disquisition.

'No data yet,' he answered. 'It is a capital mistake to theorize before you have all the evidence. It biases the judgement.'

'Is not much of it guesswork?'

'No, no: I never guess. It is a shocking habit – destructive to the logical faculty. What seems strange to you is only so because you do not follow my train of thought or observe the small facts upon which large inferences may depend. It is a mistake to confound strangeness with mystery. The most commonplace crime is often the most mysterious, because it presents no new or special features from which deductions may be drawn. As a rule, the more bizarre a thing is the less mysterious it proves to be. It is your commonplace, featureless crimes which are really puzzling, just as a commonplace face is the most difficult to identify.'

'In all crime detection there is nothing like first-hand evidence. One forms provisional theories and waits for time or fuller knowledge to explode them. One should always look for a possible alternative and provide against it. It is the first rule of criminal investigation. Circumstantial evidence is a very tricky thing: it may seem to point straight to one thing, but if you shift your own point of view a little, you may find it pointing in an equally uncompromising manner to something entirely different. It is occasionally very convincing, as when you find a trout in the milk, to quote Thoreau's example.'

Again and again Holmes impressed upon me his golden

rule in detection. 'How often have I said to you that when you have eliminated the impossible whatever remains, *however improbable*, must be the truth. It may well be that several explanations remain, in which case one tries test after test until one or other of them has a convincing amount of support.'

In some problems he said 'the grand thing is to be able to reason backwards. That is a very useful accomplishment, and a very easy one, but people do not practise it much. In the everyday affairs of life it is more useful to reason forwards, and so the other comes to be neglected. There are fifty who can reason synthetically for one who can reason analytically.'

'I confess,' said I, 'that I do not quite follow you.'

'I hardly expected that you would. Let me see if I can make it clearer. Most people, if you describe a train of events to them, will tell you what the result would be. They can put those events together in their minds, and argue from them that something will come to pass. There are few people, however, who, if you told them a result, would be able to evolve from their own inner consciousness what the steps were which led up to that result. This power is what I mean when I talk of reasoning backwards, or analytically.'

'I understand,' said I.

* * * *

'The larger crimes,' said Holmes, 'are apt to be the simpler, for the bigger the crime, the more obvious, as a rule, is the motive.'

41

He had risen from his chair, and was standing between the parted blinds, gazing down into the dull, neutral-tinted London street. 'Never trust to general impressions, my boy,' he said to me, 'but concentrate yourself upon details. My first glance is always at a woman's sleeve. In a man it is perhaps better first to take the knee of the trouser. It is an error to argue in front of your data. You find yourself insensibly twisting them to fit your theories.'

He once surprised me by saying, 'We must look for consistency. Where there is want of it we must suspect deception.'

'I hardly follow you.'

'Where a crime is coolly premeditated, then the means of covering it are coolly premeditated also.'

*　　*　　*　　*

Sherlock Holmes closed his eyes, and placed his elbows upon the arms of his chair, with his finger-tips together. 'The ideal reasoner,' he remarked, 'would, when he has once been shown a single fact in all its bearings, deduce from it not only all the chain of events which led up to it, but also all the results which would follow from it. As Cuvier could correctly describe a whole animal by the contemplation of a single bone, so the observer who has thoroughly understood one link in a series of incidents, should be able accurately to state all the other ones, both before and after. We have not yet grasped the results which the reason alone can attain to. Problems may be solved in the study which have baffled all those who have sought a solution by the aid of their senses. To carry the art, however, to its highest pitch, it is necessary that the reasoner should be able to utilize all the facts which have come to his knowledge, and this in itself implies, as you will readily see, a possession of all knowledge, which, even in these days of free education and encyclopaedias, is a somewhat rare accomplishment. It is not so impossible, however, that a man should possess all knowledge which is likely to be useful to him in his work, and this I have endeavoured in my case to do. If I remember rightly, you once defined my limits in a very precise fashion.'

'Yes,' I answered laughing. 'Philosophy, astronomy, and politics were zero, I remember. Botany variable, geology profound as regards the mudstains from any region within fifty miles of town, chemistry eccentric, anatomy unsystematic, sensational literature and crime records unique, violin player, boxer, swordsman, lawyer, and self-poisoner by cocaine and tobacco. Those, I think, were the main points of my analysis.'

Holmes grinned at the last item. 'Well,' he said, 'I say now, as I said then, that a man should keep his little brain attic stocked with all the furniture that he is likely to use, and the rest he can put away in the lumber-room of his library, where he can get it if he wants it.'

*   *   *   *

So far theory. But my friend often demonstrated his methods to me in a practical manner, as in his deduction from a battered hat left at Baker Street.

'Pray tell me, Holmes, what you can infer from this hat?'

He picked it up and gazed at it in the peculiar intro-spective fashion which was characteristic of him. 'It is perhaps less suggestive than it might have been,' he remarked, 'and yet there are a few inferences which are very distinct, and a few others which represent at least a strong balance of probability. That the man was highly intellectual is of course obvious upon the face of it, and also that he was fairly well-to-do within the last three years, although he has now fallen upon evil days. He had fore-sight, but has less now than formerly, pointing to a moral retrogression, which, taken with the decline of his fortune, seems to indicate some evil influence, probably drink, at work upon him. This may account also for the obvious fact that his wife has ceased to love him.'

'My dear Holmes!'

'He has, however, retained some degree of self-respect,' he continued, disregarding my remonstrance. 'He is a man who leads a sedentary life, goes out little, is out of training entirely, is middle-aged, has grizzled hair which he has had cut within the last few days, and which he anoints with lime-cream. These are the most patent facts which are to be deduced from his hat. Also, by the way, that it is extremely improbable that he has gas laid on in his house.'

'You are certainly joking, Holmes.'

'Not in the least. Is it possible that even now when I give you these results you are unable to see how they are attained?'

'I have no doubt that I am very stupid; but I must confess that I am unable to follow you. For example, how did you deduce that this man was intellectual?'

44

For answer Holmes clapped the hat upon his head. It came right over the forehead and settled upon the bridge of his nose. 'It is a question of cubic capacity,' said he: 'a man with so large a brain must have something in it.'*

'The decline of his fortunes, then?'

'This hat is three years old. These flat brims curled at the edge came in then. It is a hat of the very best quality. Look at the band of ribbed silk, and the excellent lining. If this man could afford to buy so expensive a hat three years ago, and has had no hat since, then he has assuredly gone down in the world.'

'Well, that is clear certainly. But how about the foresight and the moral retrogression?'

Sherlock Holmes laughed. 'Here is the foresight,' said he, putting his finger upon the little disc and loop of the hat-securer. 'They are never sold upon hats. If this man ordered one, it is a sign of a certain amount of foresight, since he went out of his way to take this precaution against the wind. But since we see that he has broken the elastic, and has not troubled to replace it, it is obvious that he has less foresight now than formerly, which is a distinct proof of a weakening nature. On the other hand, he has endeavoured to conceal some of these stains upon the felt by daubing them with ink, which is a sign that he has not entirely lost his self-respect.'

'Your reasoning is certainly plausible.'

'The further points, that he is middle-aged, that his hair is grizzled, that it has been recently cut, and that he uses

---

* If the hat came down to Holmes's nose the owner's head must been enormous or Holmes's own head small. But according to Watson he had one of the finest brains of the age – EDITOR.

lime-cream, are all to be gathered from a close examination of the lower part of the lining. The lens discloses a large number of hair-ends, clean cut by the scissors of the barber. They all appear to be adhesive, and there is a distinct odour of lime-cream. This dust, you will observe, is not the gritty, grey dust of the street, but the fluffy brown dust of the house, showing that it has been hung up indoors most of the time; while the marks of moisture upon the inside are proof positive that the wearer perspired very freely, and could, therefore, hardly be in the best of training.'

'But his wife – you said that she had ceased to love him.'

'This hat has not been brushed for weeks. When I see a man, my dear Watson, with a week's accumulation of dust upon his hat, and when his wife allows him to go out in such a state, I fear that he has been unfortunate enough to lose his wife's affections.'

'But he might be a bachelor.'

'Nay, remember that he was bringing home a goose as a peace-offering to his wife.'

'You have an answer to everything. But how on earth do you deduce that the gas is not laid on in the house?'

'One tallow stain, or even two, might come by chance; but, when I see no less than five, I think that there can be little doubt that the individual must be brought into frequent contact with burning tallow – walks upstairs at night probably with his hat in one hand and a guttered candle in the other. Anyhow, he never got tallow stains from a gas jet. Are you satisfied?'

* * * *

I remember how the sinister Baskerville case opened with a remarkable deduction by Holmes from our client's walking-stick. Holmes, who was usually very late in the mornings, save upon those not infrequent occasions when he stayed up all night, was seated at the breakfast table. I stood upon the hearth-rug and picked up the stick which our visitor had left behind him the night before. It was a fine, thick piece of wood, bulbous-headed, of the sort which is known as 'Penang lawyer'. Just under the head was a broad silver band, nearly an inch across. 'To James Mortimer, M.R.C.S., from his friends of the C.C.H.', was engraved upon it, with the date '1884'. It was just such a stick as the old-fashioned family practitioner used to carry – dignified, solid, reassuring.

'Well, Watson, what do you make of it?'

Holmes was sitting with his back to me, and I had given him no sign of my occupation.

'How did you know what I was doing? I believe you have eyes in the back of your head.'

'I have, at least, a well-polished silver-plated coffee-pot in front of me,' said he. 'But, tell me, Watson, what do you make of our visitor's stick? Let me hear you recon- struct the man by an examination of it.'

'I think,' said I, following so far as I could the methods of my companion, 'that Dr. Mortimer is a successful elderly medical man, well-esteemed, since those who know him give him this mark of their appreciation.'

'Good!' said Holmes. 'Excellent!'

'I think also that the probability is in favour of his being a country practitioner who does a great deal of his visiting on foot.'

'Why so?'

'Because this stick, though originally a very handsome one, has been so knocked about that I can hardly imagine a town practitioner carrying it. The thick iron ferrule is worn down, so it is evident that he has done a great amount of walking with it.'

'Perfectly sound!' said Holmes.

'And then again, there is the "friends of the C.C.H.". I should guess that to be the Something Hunt, the local hunt to whose members he has possibly given some surgical assistance, and which has made him a small presentation in return.'

'Really, Watson, you excel yourself,' said Holmes pushing back his chair. 'I am bound to say that in all the accounts which you have been so good as to give of my own small achievements you have habitually underrated your own abilities. It may be that you are not yourself luminous, but you are a conductor of light. Some people without possessing genius have a remarkable power of stimulating it. I confess, my dear fellow, that I am very much in your debt.'

He had never said as much before, and I must admit that his words gave me keen pleasure, for I had often been piqued by his indifference to my admiration and to the attempts which I had made to give publicity to his methods. I was proud, too, to think that I had so far mastered his system as to apply it in a way which earned his approval. He now took the stick from my hands and examined it for a few minutes with his naked eyes. Then, with an expression of interest, and carrying the cape to the window, he looked over it again with a convex lens.

48

'Interesting, though elementary,' said he, as he returned to his favourite corner of the settee. 'There are certainly one or two indications upon the stick. It gives us the basis for several deductions.'

'Has anything escaped me?' I asked, with some self-importance. 'I trust that there is nothing of consequence which I have overlooked?'

'I am afraid, my dear Watson, that most of your conclusions were erroneous. When I said that you stimulated me I meant, to be frank, that in noting your fallacies I was occasionally guided towards the truth. Not that you are entirely wrong in this instance. The man is certainly a country practitioner. And he walks a good deal.'

'Then I was right.'

'To that extent.'

'But that was all.'

'No, no my dear Watson, not all – by no means all. I would suggest, for example, that a presentation to a doctor is more likely to come from a hospital than from a hunt, and that when the initials "C.C." are placed before that hospital the words "Charing Cross" very naturally suggest themselves.'

'You may be right.'

'The probability lies in that direction. And if we take this as a working hypothesis we have a fresh basis from which to start our construction of this unknown visitor.'

'Well, then, supposing that "C.C.H." does stand for "Charing Cross Hospital", what further inferences may we draw?'

'Do none suggest themselves? You know my methods. Apply them!'

49

'I can only think of the obvious conclusion that the man has practised in town before going to the country.'

'I think we might venture a little farther than this. Look at it in this light. On what occasion would it be most probable that such a presentation would be made? When would his friends unite to give him a pledge of their good will? Obviously at the moment when Dr. Mortimer withdrew from the service of the hospital in order to start in practice for himself. We know there has been a presentation. We believe there has been a change from a town hospital to a country practice. Is it, then, stretching our inference too far to say that the presentation was on the occasion of the change?'

'It certainly seems probable.'

'Now, you will observe that he could not have been on the *staff* of the hospital, since only a man well-established in a London practice could hold such a position, and such a one would not drift into the country. What was he, then? If he was in the hospital and yet not on the staff, he could only have been a house-surgeon or a house-physician – little more than a senior student. And he left five years ago – the date is on the stick. So your grave, middle-aged family practitioner vanishes into thin air, my dear Watson, and there emerges a young fellow under thirty, amiable, unambitious, absent-minded, and the possessor of a favourite dog, which I should describe roughly as being larger than a terrier and smaller than a mastiff.'

I laughed incredulously as Sherlock Holmes leaned back in his settee and blew little wavering rings of smoke up to the ceiling.

'As to the latter part, I have no means of checking

you,' said I, 'but at least it is not difficult to find out a few particulars about the man's age and professional career.'

From my small medical shelf I took down the Medical Directory and turned up the name. There were several Mortimers, but only one who could be our visitor. I read his record aloud.

'Mortimer, James, M.R.C.S., 1882, Grimpen, Dartmoor, Devon. House-surgeon, from 1882 to 1884, at Charing Cross Hospital. Winner of the Jackson Prize for Comparative Pathology, with essay entitled, "Is Disease a Reversion?" Corresponding member of the Swedish Pathological Society. Author of "Some Freaks of Atavism" (*Lancet*, 1882), "Do we Progress?" (*Journal of Psychology*, March, 1883). Medical Officer for the parishes of Grimpen, Thorsley, and High Barrow.'

'No mention of that local hunt, Watson,' said Holmes, with a mischievous smile, 'but a country doctor, as you very astutely observed. I think that I am fairly justified in my inferences. As to the adjectives, I said, if I remember right, amiable, unambitious, and absent-minded. It is my experience that it is only an amiable man in this world who receives testimonials, only an unambitious one who abandons a London career for the country and only an absent-minded one who leaves his stick and not his visiting-card after waiting an hour in your room.'

'And the dog?'

'Has been in the habit of carrying this stick behind his master. Being a heavy stick the dog has held it tightly by the middle, and the marks of his teeth are very plainly visible. The dog's jaw, as shown in the space between these marks, is too broad in my opinion for a terrier and not broad enough for a mastiff. It may have been a curly-haired spaniel' – as indeed we found it to be when Dr. Mortimer returned with such a dog.

*   *   *   *

On another occasion Holmes made a remarkable series of deductions from an old pipe left behind by a client.

'A nice old briar with a good long stem of what the tobacconists call amber. I wonder how many real amber mouthpieces there are in London. Some people think a fly in it is a sign. Why, it is quite a branch of trade, the putting of sham flies into the sham amber. Well, he must have been disturbed in his mind to leave a pipe behind him which he evidently values highly.'

'How do you know that he values it highly?' I asked.

'Well, I should put the original cost of the pipe at seven-and-sixpence. Now it has, you see, been twice mended: once in the wooden stem and once in the amber. Each of these mends, done, as you observe, with silver bands, must have cost more than the pipe did originally. The man must value the pipe highly when he prefers to patch it up rather than buy a new one with the same money.'

'Anything else?' I asked, for Holmes was turning the pipe about in his hand and staring at it in his peculiar pensive way.

He held it up and tapped it with his long, thin forefinger as a professor might who was lecturing on a bone.

'Pipes are occasionally of extraordinary interest,' said he. 'Nothing has more individuality save, perhaps, watches and bootlaces. The indications here, however, are neither very marked nor very important. The owner is obviously a muscular man, left-handed, with an excellent set of teeth, careless in his habits, and with no need to practise economy.'

My friend threw out the information in a very off-hand way, but I saw that he cocked his eye at me to see if I had followed his reasoning.

'You think a man must be well-to-do if he smokes a seven-shilling pipe?' said I.

'This is Grosvenor mixture at eightpence an ounce,' Holmes answered, knocking a little out on his palm. 'As he might get an excellent smoke for half the price, he has no need to practise economy.'*

'And the other points?'

'He has been at the habit of lighting his pipe at lamps and gas-jets. You can see that it is quite charred all down one side. Of course, a match could not have done that. Why should a man hold a match to the side of his pipe? But you cannot light it at a lamp without getting the bowl charred. And it is on the right side of the pipe. From that I gather that he is a left-handed man. You hold your own pipe to the lamp, and see how naturally you, being right-handed, hold the left side to the flame. You might do it once the other way, but not as a constancy. This has always been held so. Then he has bitten through

* Today this 7s. pipe would cost about £3. The best tobacco is about 9s. an ounce, and 'an excellent smoke' cannot be had for less than 6s. an ounce – EDITOR.

his amber. It takes a muscular, energetic fellow, and one with a good set of teeth to do that.'

Holmes had made a minute study of tobacco ash, and had written a monograph 'Upon the Distinction Between the Ashes of the Various Tobaccos'. 'In it,' he said, 'I enumerate a hundred and forty forms of cigar, cigarette, and pipe tobacco, with coloured plates illustrating the difference in the ash. I flatter myself that I can distinguish at a glance the ash of any known brand either of cigar or of tobacco. It is a point which is continually turning up in criminal trials, and which is sometimes of supreme importance as a clue. If you can say definitely, for example, that some murder had been done by a man who was smoking an Indian lunkah, it obviously narrows your field of search. To the trained eye there is as much difference between the black ash of a Trichinopoly and the white fluff of bird's-eye as there is between a cabbage and a potato.'

'You have an extraordinary genius for minutiae,' I remarked.

'I appreciate their importance. Here is my monograph upon the tracing of footsteps, with some remarks upon the uses of plaster of Paris as a preserver of impresses. Here, too, is a curious little work upon the influence of a trade upon the form of the hand, with lithotypes of the hands of slaters, sailors, cork-cutters, compositors, weavers, and diamond-polishers. That is a matter of great practical interest to the scientific detective – especially in cases of unclaimed bodies, or in discovering the antecedents of criminals.'

*   *   *   *

Holmes and I sat together in silence all the evening, he engaged with a powerful lens deciphering the remains of the original inscription upon a palimpsest, I deep in a recent treatise upon surgery.

'Well, Watson, it's as well we have not to turn out tonight,' said Holmes, laying aside his lens and rolling up the palimpsest. 'I've done enough for one sitting. It is trying work for the eyes. So far as I can make out, it is nothing more exciting than an Abbey's accounts dating from the second half of the fifteenth century.'

It was an instructive sight to see Holmes working on a problem. I once watched him for two hours trying to unravel a cipher as he covered sheet after sheet of paper with figures and letters, so completely absorbed in his task that he had evidently forgotten my presence. Sometimes he was making progress, and whistled and sang at his work; sometimes he was puzzled and would sit for a long spell with a furrowed brow and a vacant eye. Finally he sprang from his chair with a cry of satisfaction, and walked up and down the room rubbing his hands together. 'I am fairly familiar with all forms of secret writing,' he told me, 'and am myself the author of a trifling monograph upon the subject in which I analyse one hundred and sixty separate ciphers. What one man can invent another can discover.'

Another of my friend's many interests was printer's type. 'There is as much difference to my eye between the leaded bourgeois type of a *Times* article and the slovenly print of an evening halfpenny newspaper as there could be between your Negro and your Esquimaux. The detection of types is one of the most elementary branches of knowledge to the special expert in crime, though I confess that once when I was a very young man I confused the *Leeds Mercury* with the *Western Morning News*. But a *Times* leader is entirely distinctive.'

Tobacco ash, footcasts, printer's type – nothing was too small to escape my friend's notice. 'You will remember, Watson, how the dreadful business of the Abernetty family was first brought to my notice by the depth which the parsley had sunk into the butter upon a hot day.'

* * * *

There was a good deal of the actor in Holmes, indeed he once said to me, 'The best way of successfully acting a part is to be it.' He was a master of disguise and make-up and acted upon his own maxim. Disguised as a seedy groom in the Irene Adler case he completely baffled me. One afternoon the door opened and a drunken-looking, ill-kempt and side-whiskered groom with an inflamed face and disreputable clothes walked in. Accustomed as I was to my friend's amazing powers in the use of disguises, I had to look three times before I was certain that it was indeed he. When in the Milverton case he had to become a work man and make love to a servant he so far became the man as to take in the girl completely. Servants were for him a valuable source of evidence. 'There are no better instruments than discharged servants with a grievance,' he said.

Perhaps his most remarkable disguise was in the singular case which I have called 'The Man with the Twisted Lip', when he became a filthy old opium-smoking wreck in a

"Upper Swandham Lane"
(*Mansell Collection*)

den in Upper Swandham Lane – a foul alley, lurking behind the high wharves which line the north side of the river to the east of London Bridge, between a slop shop and a gin shop. I remember that the den was approached by a steep flight of stairs leading down to a black gap like the mouth of a cave. When he revealed himself, it took all my self-control to prevent me from breaking out into a cry of astonishment.

Holmes could find his way into the remotest corners of London. 'It is a hobby of mine to have an exact knowledge of London,' he said. He was helped by a team of quick-witted street urchins who acted as his informants, his 'eyes' on the metropolis – the 'Baker Street Irregulars' as we called them.

But though his knowledge of London was remarkable, he showed little knowledge or appreciation of the country-side. I once praised the red and grey roofs of the farm-steadings peeping out from amidst the light green of the foliage.

'Are they not fresh and beautiful?'

Holmes shook his head gravely.

'Do you know, Watson, that it is one of the curses of a mind with a turn like mine that I must look at everything with reference to my own subject. You look at country cottages and you are impressed by their beauty. I look at them, and the only thought that which comes to me is a feeling of their isolation, and of the impunity with which crime may be committed there.'

'Good heavens!' I cried. 'Who would associate crime with such dear little homesteads?'

'They always fill me with a certain horror. It is my

belief, Watson, founded upon my experience, that the lowest and vilest alleys in London do not present a more dreadful record of sin than does the smiling and beautiful countryside.'*

'You horrify me!'

'But the reason is very obvious. The pressure of public opinion can do in the town what the law cannot accomplish. There is no lane so vile that the scream of a tortured child, or the thud of a drunkard's blow, does not beget sympathy and indignation among the neighbours, and then the whole machinery of justice is ever so close that a word of complaint can set it going, and there is but a step between the crime and the dock. But look at these lonely houses, each in its own fields, filled for the most part with poor ignorant folk who know little of the law. Think of the deeds of hellish cruelty, the hidden wickedness which may go on, year in, year out, in such places, and none the wiser.'

Sometimes the only clue to trouble in a lonely house is a barking dog. Holmes observed dogs closely. 'A dog reflects the family life. Whoever saw a frisky dog in a gloomy family, or a sad dog in a happy one? Snarling people have snarling dogs, dangerous people have dangerous ones. And their passing moods may reflect the passing moods of others. I have serious thoughts of writing a small monograph upon the uses of dogs in the work of the detective.'

* Holmes was exaggerating. But H. V. Morton in *In Search of England* (p. 88 of 21st edn.) recounts a conversation he had with the elderly vicar of an exquisitely beautiful and remote village. Morton took Watson's view. but the vicar inclined more to that of Holmes. 'Oh yes, there is sin here,' he said. 'Indeed there is sin' – EDITOR

I recalled our terrible experience with the Baskerville hound. But Holmes reminded me of another episode when he drew a police inspector's attention to the importance of the dog that did not bark.

'May I draw your attention to the curious incident of the dog in the night-time.'

'The dog did nothing in the night-time.'

'That was the curious incident,' remarked Sherlock Holmes.

ON HUMAN NATURE

It was the end of November, and Holmes and I sat, upon a raw and foggy night, on either side of a blazing fire in our sitting-room in Baker Street. He had been engaged in two affairs of the utmost importance, in the first of which he had exposed the atrocious conduct of Colonel Upwood in connection with the famous card scandal of the Nonpareil Club, while in the second he had defended the unfortunate Mme Montpensier from the charge of murder which hung over her in connection with the death of her step-daughter, Mlle Carere, the young lady who was found six months later alive and married in New York.

'My dear fellow,' said Sherlock Holmes, 'life is infinitely stranger than anything which the mind of man could invent. We would not dare to conceive the things which are really mere commonplaces of existence. If we could fly out of that window hand in hand, hover over this great city, gently remove the roofs, and peep in at the queer things which are going on, the strange coincidences, the plannings, the cross-purposes, the wonderful chains of events, working through generations, and leading to the most *outré* results, it would make all fiction with its conventionalities and foreseen conclusions most stale and unprofitable.'

'And yet I am not convinced of it,' I answered. 'The cases which come to light in the papers are, as a rule, bald enough, and vulgar enough. We have in our police reports, realism pushed to its extreme limits, and yet the result is, it must be confessed, neither fascinating nor artistic.'

'A certain selection and discretion must be used in producing a realistic effect,' remarked Holmes. 'This is wanting in the police report, where more stress is laid perhaps upon the platitudes of the magistrate than upon the details, which to an observer contain the vital essence of the whole matter. Depend upon it there is nothing so unnatural as the commonplace.'

I smiled and shook my head. 'I can quite understand you thinking so,' I said. 'Of course, in your position of unofficial adviser and helper to everybody who is ab-solutely puzzled, throughout three continents, you are brought in contact with all that is strange and bizarre. But here' – I picked up the morning paper from the ground – 'let us put it to a practical test. Here is the first heading upon which I come. "A husband's cruelty to his wife." There is half a column of print, but I know without reading it that it is all perfectly familiar to me. There is, of course, the other woman, the drink, the push, the blow, the bruise, the sympathetic sister or landlady. The crudest of writers could invent nothing more crude.'

'Indeed, your example is an unfortunate one for your argument,' said Holmes, taking up the paper, and glancing his eye down it. 'This is the Dundas separation case, and, as it happens, I was engaged in clearing up some small points in connection with it. The husband was a tee-totaller, there was no other woman, and the conduct complained of was that he had drifted into the habit of winding up every meal by taking out his false teeth and hurling them at his wife, which you will allow is not an action likely to occur to the imagination of the average story-teller. Take a pinch of snuff, Doctor, and acknowledge that I have scored over you in your example.'

He held out a snuff-box of old gold, with a great amethyst in the centre of the lid. Its splendour was in such contrast to his homely ways and simple life that I could not help commenting upon it.

'It is a little souvenir from the King of Bohemia.'

'And the ring?' I asked, glancing at a remarkable brilliant that sparkled upon his finger.

'It was from the reigning family of Holland, though the matter in which I served them was of such delicacy that I cannot confide it even to you.'

* * * *

'A strange enigma is man,' said Sherlock Holmes.

'Someone calls him a soul concealed in an animal,' I suggested.

'Winwood Reade is good upon the subject,' said Holmes. 'He remarks that, while the individual man is an insoluble puzzle, in the aggregate he becomes a mathematical certainty. You can, for example, never foretell what any one man will do, but you can say with precision what an average number will be up to. Individuals vary, but percentages remain constant. So says the statistician.'

* * * *

I sometimes found myself regarding Sherlock Holmes as an isolated phenomenon, a brain without a heart, as deficient in human sympathy as he was pre-eminent in intelligence. His aversion to women, and his disinclination to form new friendships, were both typical of his unemotional character, but not more so than his complete suppression of every reference to his own people. I had come to believe that he was an orphan with no relatives living, but one day, to my very great surprise, he began to talk to me about his brother.

It was after tea on a summer evening, and the conversation, which had roamed in a desultory, spasmodic fashion from golf clubs to the causes of the change in the obliquity of the ecliptic,* came round at last to the question of atavism and hereditary aptitudes. The point under discussion was how far any singular gift in an individual was due to his ancestry, and how far to his own early training.

'In your own case,' said I, 'from all that you have told me it seems obvious that your faculty of observation and your peculiar facility for deduction are due to your own systematic training.'

'To some extent,' he answered, thoughtfully. 'My ancestors were country squires, who appear to have led much the same life as is natural to their class. But, none the less, my turn that way is in my veins, and may have come with my grandmother, who was the sister of Vernet, the French artist. Art in the blood is liable to take the strangest forms.'

'But how do you know that it is hereditary?'

'Because my brother Mycroft possesses it in a larger degree than I do.'

---

* Holmes's comments on this must have been illuminating in view of his supposed ignorance of the Copernican Theory – EDITOR.

This was news to me indeed. If there were another man with such singular powers in England, how was it that neither police nor public had heard of him? I put the question, with a hint that it was my companion's modesty which made him acknowledge his brother as his superior. Holmes laughed at my suggestion.

'My dear Watson,' said he. 'I cannot agree with those who rank modesty among the virtues. To the logician all things should be seen exactly as they are, and to underestimate oneself is as much a departure from truth as to exaggerate one's own powers. When I say, therefore, that Mycroft has better powers of observation than I, you may take it that I am speaking the exact and literal truth.

'Is he your junior?'

'Seven years my senior.'

'How comes it that he is unknown?'

'Oh, he is very well known in his own circle.'

'Where, then?'

'Well, in the Diogenes Club, for example.'

I had never heard of the institution, and my face must have proclaimed as much.

'You wonder why it is that Mycroft does not use his powers for detective work. He is incapable of it.'

'But I thought you said —!'

'I said that he was my superior in observation and deduction. If the art of the detective began and ended in reasoning from an arm-chair, my brother would be the greatest criminal agent that ever lived. But he has no ambition and no energy. He would not even go out of his way to verify his own solutions, and would rather be considered wrong than take the trouble to prove himself right. Again and again I have taken a problem to him and have received an explanation which has afterwards proved to be the correct one. And yet he was absolutely incapable of working out the practical points which must be gone into before a case could be laid before a judge or jury.'

'It is not his profession, then?'

'By no means. What is to me a means of livelihood is to him the merest hobby of a dilettante. He has an extraordinary faculty for figures, and audits the books in some of the Government departments. Mycroft lodges in Pall Mall, and he walks round the corner into Whitehall every morning and back every evening. From year's end to year's end he takes no other exercise, and is seen nowhere else, except only in the Diogenes Club, which is just opposite his rooms.'

'I cannot recall the name.'

'Very likely not. There are many men in London, you know, who, some from shyness, some from misanthropy have no wish for the company of their fellows. Yet they are not averse to comfortable chairs and the latest periodicals. It is for the convenience of these that the Diogenes Club was started, and it now contains the most unsociable and unclubbable men in town. No member is permitted to take the least notice of any other one. My brother was one of the founders.'

'You said he had some small office under the British Government.'

Holmes chuckled. 'You are right in thinking that he is under the British Government. You would also be right in a sense if you said that occasionally he *is* the British Government.'

'My dear Holmes!'

'I thought I might surprise you. Mycroft draws four hundred and fifty pounds a year, remains a subordinate, has no ambitions of any kind, will receive neither honour nor title, but remains the most indispensable man in the country.'

'But how?'

'Well, his position is unique. He has made it for himself. There has never been anything like it before, nor will be again. He has the tidiest and most orderly brain, with the greatest capacity for storing facts, of any man living. All other men are specialists, but his specialism is omniscience. In that great brain of his, everything is pigeon-holed, and can be handed out in an instant. Again and again his word has decided national policy. He lives in it. He thinks of nothing else save when, as an intellectual exercise, he unbends if I call upon him and ask him to advise me on one of my little problems.'

*   *   *   *

If Mycroft Holmes was a super-intelligence directed to moral ends, Professor Moriarty was his opposite number.

'I could not sit quiet in my chair, Watson, if I thought that such a man as Professor Moriarty were walking the streets of London unchallenged.'

'What has he done, then?'

'His career has been an extraordinary one. He is a man of good birth and excellent education, endowed by nature with a phenomenal mathematical faculty. At the age of

66

twenty-one he wrote a treatise upon the Binomial Theorem, which has had a European vogue.* On the strength of it, he won the Mathematical Chair at one of our smaller Universities, and had, to all appearances, a most brilliant career before him. But the man had hereditary tendencies of the most diabolical kind. A criminal strain ran in his blood, which, instead of being modified, was increased and rendered infinitely more dangerous by his extraordinary mental powers. Dark rumours gathered round him in the University town, and eventually he was compelled to resign his Chair and to come down to London, where he set up as an Army coach. So much is known to the world, but what I am telling you now is what I have myself discovered.

'As you are aware, Watson, there is no one who knows the higher criminal world of London so well as I do. For years past I have continually been conscious of some power behind the malefactor, some deep organizing power which for ever stands in the way of the law, and throws its shield over the wrongdoer. Again and again in cases of the most varying sorts – forgery cases, robberies, murders – I have felt the presence of this force, and I have deduced its action in many of those undiscovered crimes in which I have not been personally consulted. For years I have endeavoured to break through the veil which shrouded it, and at last the time came when I seized my thread and followed it, until it led me, after a thousand cunning windings, to ex-Professor Moriarty of mathematical celebrity.

* The Binomial Theorem is beautiful and useful, but it is difficult to see how Moriarty could have thrown any new light upon it – EDITOR.

'He is the Napoleon of crime, Watson. He is the organizer of half that is evil and of nearly all that is undetected in this great city. He is a genius, a philosopher, an abstract thinker. He has a brain of the first order. He sits motionless, like a spider in the centre of its web, but that web has a thousand radiations, and he knows well every quiver of each of them. He does little himself. He only plans. But his agents are numerous and splendidly organized. Is there a crime to be done, a paper to be abstracted, we will say, a house to be rifled, a man to be removed – the word is passed to the Professor, the matter is organized and carried out. The agent may be caught. In that case money is found for his bail or his defence. But the central power which uses the agent is never caught – never so much as suspected. This was the organization which I deduced, Watson, and which I devoted my whole energy to exposing and breaking up.

'But the Professor was fenced round with safeguards, so cunningly devised that, do what I would, it seemed impossible to get evidence which could convict in a court of law. You know my powers, my dear Watson, and yet at the end of three months I was forced to confess that I had at last met an antagonist who was my intellectual equal. My horror at his crimes was lost in my admiration at his skill. But at last he made a trip – only a little trip – but it was more than he could afford, when I was so close upon him. I had my chance, and, starting from that point, I have woven my net round him until now it is all ready to close.

'The greatest schemer of all time, the organizer of every devilry, the controlling brain of the underworld – a brain which might have made or marred the destiny of nations. That's the man. But so aloof is he from general suspicion – so immune from criticism – so admirable in his management and self-effacement, that for my words of criticism he could haul me before a court and emerge the winner. In his book *The Dynamics of an Asteroid* he ascends to such rarefied heights of pure mathematics that it is said that there was no man in the scientific press capable of criticizing it. Is this a man to traduce? Foul-mouthed detective and slandered professor – such would be our respective roles. That's genius, Watson.

'I must tell you, Watson, that the man, knowing he was cornered, called on me. My nerves are fairly proof, but I must confess to a start when I saw the very man who has been so much in my thoughts standing there on my threshold. He is extremely tall and thin, his forehead domes out in a white curve, and his two eyes are deeply sunken in his head. He is clean-shaven, pale, and ascetic-looking, retaining something of the professor in his features. His shoulders are rounded from much study, and his face protrudes forward, and is for ever slowly oscillating from side to side in a curious reptilian fashion. I confess he left an unpleasant effect upon my mind. His soft, precise fashion of speech leaves a conviction of sincerity which a mere bully could not produce.

'He has already acted. I have been attacked by a two-horse van dashing furiously round a corner, and later in the day by a rough with a bludgeon.*

*P. G. Wodehouse, in an article in *Punch*, (1955), comments: 'A rough with a bludgeon! Gad, sir, if I were a fiend in human shape with a brain of the first order I would think up something a little better than roughs with bludgeons.'

'I happen to know the first link in the Moriarty chain. His chief of the staff is Colonel Sebastian Moran, as aloof and guarded and inaccessible to the law as himself. What do you think he pays him?'

'I'd like to hear.'

'Six thousand a year. That's paying for brains, you see – the American business principle. That gives you an idea of Moriarty's gains and of the great scale on which he works. Another point. I made it my business to hunt down some of Moriarty's cheques lately – just common innocent cheques that he pays his household bills with. They were drawn on six different banks. Does that make any impression on your mind?'

'Queer, certainly. But what do you gather from it?'

'That he wanted no gossip about his wealth. No single man should know what he had. Some time when you have a year or two to spare I commend to you the study of Professor Moriarty.'

*   *   *   *

'Just give me down my index of biographies from the shelf, Watson.' Holmes turned over the pages lazily, leaning back in his chair and blowing great clouds of smoke from his cigar.

'My collection of M's is a fine one,' said he. 'Moriarty himself is enough to make any letter illustrious, and here is Morgan the poisoner, and Merridew of abominable memory, and Mathews who knocked out my left canine in the waiting-room at Charing Cross, and, finally here is Colonel Moran.'

He handed me over the book, and I read: '*Moran, Sebastian, Colonel*. Unemployed. Formerly 1st Bengalore Pioneers. Born London, 1840. Son of Sir Augustus Moran, C.B., once British Minister to Persia. Educated Eton and Oxford. Served in Jowaki Campaign, Afghan Campaign, Charasiab (dispatches), Sherpur, and Cabul. Author of *Heavy Game of the Western Himalayas*, 1881; *Three Months in the Jungle*, 1884. Address: Conduit Street. Clubs: The Anglo-Indian, the Tankerville, the Bagatelle Card Club.'

On the margin was written in Holmes's precise hand: 'The second most dangerous man in London.'

'This is astonishing,' said I, as I handed back the volume. 'The man's career is that of an honourable soldier.'

'It is true,' Holmes answered. 'Up to a certain point he did well. He was always a man of iron nerve, and the story is still told in India how he crawled down a drain after a wounded man-eating tiger. There are some trees, Watson, which grow to a certain height and then suddenly develop some unsightly eccentricity. You will see it often in humans. I have a theory that the individual represents in his development the whole procession of his ancestors, and that such a sudden turn to good or evil stands for some strong influence which came into the line of his pedigree. The person becomes, as it were, the epitome of the history of his own family.'

'It is surely rather fanciful.'

'Well, I don't insist upon it. Whatever the cause, Colonel Moran began to go wrong. Without any open scandal, he still made India too hot to hold him. He retired, came to London, and again acquired an evil name. It was at this time that he was sought out by Professor Moriarty, to whom for a time he was chief of the staff.'

*   *   *   *

But of all the criminals with whom Holmes dealt, Charles Augustus Milverton, the blackmailer, filled him with the greatest loathing. 'He is the worst man in London,' said Holmes. 'Do you feel a creeping sensation, Watson, when you stand before the serpents in the Zoo and see the slithery, gliding, venomous creatures, with their deadly eyes and wicked, flattened faces? Well, that's how Milverton impresses me. I've had to do with fifty murderers in my career, but the worst of them never gave me the repulsion which I have for this fellow.'

'But who is he?'

'I'll tell you, Watson. He is the king of all the black-mailers. Heaven help the man, and still more the woman, whose secret and reputation come into the power of Milverton. With a smiling face and a heart of marble he will squeeze and squeeze until he has drained them dry. The fellow is a genius in his way, and would have made his mark in some more savoury trade. His method is as follows: He allows it to be known that he is prepared to pay very high sums for letters which compromise people of wealth or position. He receives these wares not only from treacherous valets or maids, but frequently from genteel ruffians who have gained the confidence and affection of trusting women. He deals with no niggard hand. I happen to know that he paid seven hundred pounds to a footman for a note two lines in length, and that the ruin of a noble family was the result. Everything which is in the market goes to Milverton, and there are hundreds in this great city who turn white at his name. No one knows where his grip may fall, for he is far too rich and far too cunning to work from hand to mouth. He will hold a card back for years in order to play it at the moment when the stake is best worth winning. I have said that he is the worst man in London, and I would ask you how could one compare the ruffian who in hot blood bludgeons his mate with this man, who methodically and at his leisure tortures the soul and wrings the nerves in order to add to his already swollen money-bags?'

I had seldom heard my friend speak with such intensity of feeling.

'But surely,' said I, 'the fellow must be within the grasp of the law?'

'Technically, no doubt, but practically not. What would it profit a woman, for example, to get him a few months' imprisonment if her own ruin must immediately follow?* His victims dare not hit back. If ever he blackmailed an innocent person, then, indeed we should have him; but he is as cunning as the Evil One.'

*   *   *   *

Holmes's knowledge of crime extended from individuals to secret societies. 'Have you never heard,' he said to me, bending forward and sinking his voice, 'of the Ku Klux Klan?'

---

* The laws against blackmail must have changed since Holmes's time. Today it would be years – EDITOR.

'I never have.'

Holmes turned over the leaves of a book upon his knee. 'Here it is,' said he presently, '"Ku Klux Klan. A name derived from a fanciful resemblance to the sound produced by cocking a rifle. This terrible secret society was formed by some ex-Confederate soldiers in the Southern States after the Civil War, and it rapidly formed local branches in different parts of the country, notably in Tennessee, Louisiana, the Carolinas, Georgia, and Florida. Its power was used for political purposes, principally for the terrorizing of the Negro voters, and the murdering or driving from the country of those who were opposed to its views. Its outrages were usually preceded by a warning sent to the marked man in some fantastic but generally recognized shape – a sprig of oak leaves in some parts, melon seeds or orange pips in others. On receiving this the victim might either openly abjure his former ways, or might fly from the country. If he braved the matter out, death would unfailingly come upon him, and usually in some strange and unforeseen manner. So perfect was the organization of the society, and so systematic its methods, that there is hardly a case upon record where any man succeeded in braving it with impunity, or in which any of its outrages were traced home to the perpetrators. For some years the organization flourished, in spite of the efforts of the United States Government, and of the better classes of the community in the South. Eventually, in the year 1869, the movement rather suddenly collapsed, although there have been sporadic outbursts of the same sort since that date."'

*　　*　　*　　*

It was the third week in November and a dense yellow fog settled down upon London. From the Monday to the Thursday I doubt whether it was possible from our windows in Baker Street to see the loom of the opposite houses. The first day Holmes had spent in cross-indexing his huge book of references. The second and third had been patiently occupied upon a subject which he had recently made his hobby – the music of the Middle Ages. But when, for the fourth time, after pushing back our chairs from breakfast we saw the greasy, heavy brown swirl still drifting past us and condensing in oily drops upon the window-panes, my comrade's impatient and active nature could endure this drab existence no longer. He paced restlessly about our sitting-room in a fever of suppressed energy, biting his nails, tapping the furniture, and chafing against inaction.

'Nothing of interest in the paper, Watson?' he asked.

I was aware that by anything of interest, Holmes meant anything of criminal interest. There was the news of a revolution, of a possible war, and of an impending change of Government; but these did not come within the horizon of my companion. I could see nothing recorded in the shape of crime which was not commonplace and futile. Holmes groaned and resumed his restless meanderings.

'The London criminal is certainly a dull fellow,' said he, in the querulous voice of the sportsman whose game has failed him. 'Look out of this window, Watson. See how the figures loom up, are dimly seen, and then blend once more into the cloud-bank. The thief or the murderer could roam London on such a day as the tiger does the jungle, unseen until he pounces, and then evident only to his victim.'

'There have,' said I, 'been numerous petty thefts.'

Holmes snorted his contempt.

'This great and sombre stage is set for something more worthy than that,' said he. 'It is fortunate for this community that I am not a criminal.'

'Nor me.'

'Yes,' said Holmes. 'When a doctor does go wrong he is the first of criminals. He has the nerve and he has the knowledge. Palmer and Pritchard were among the heads of their profession.'

The conversation drifted around to the deceptive appearance of some criminals. 'Sometimes,' I said, 'a man's appearance will go far with a jury.'

'That is a dangerous argument, my dear Watson. You remember that terrible murderer, Bert Stevens, who wanted us to get him off in '87. Was there ever a more mild-mannered, Sunday-school young man?'

On the charm of many criminals he said, 'Some people's affability is more deadly than the violence of coarser souls.'

He believed firmly in the law of natural retribution. 'The wages of sin, Watson – the wages of sin! Sooner or later it will always come.'

*　　*　　*　　*

My friend often noted the strange attraction of sinful men for good women. 'You may have noticed how extremes to each other, the spiritual to the animal, the cave-man to the angel.'

Women were an enigma to him. 'I am not a whole-souled admirer of womankind, as you are aware, Watson. Love is an emotional thing, and whatever is emotional is opposed to that true, cold reason which I place above all things. I should never marry myself, lest I bias my judgement. Women are never to be trusted entirely – not the best of them.'

I did not pause to argue over this atrocious sentiment.

He observed women closely. 'Oscillation upon the pavement always means an *affaire du coeur*. When a woman has been seriously wronged by a man she no longer oscillates, and the usual symptom is a broken bell-wire.'

Once when a pre-paid telegram arrived. I asked, 'Man or woman?'

'Oh, man, of course. No woman would ever send a reply-paid telegram. She would have come.'

'One of the most dangerous classes in the world,' said he, 'is the drifting and friendless woman. She is the most harmless, and often the most useful of mortals, but she is the inevitable inciter of crime in others. She is helpless. She is migratory. She has sufficient means to take her from country to country and from hotel to hotel. She is lost, as often as not, in a maze of obscure *pensions* and boarding houses. She is a stray chicken in a world of foxes. When she is gobbled up she is hardly missed.'

I think he had a soft spot for our landlady, Mrs. Hudson – or for her cooking.

'Mrs. Hudson has risen to the occasion,' said Holmes uncovering a dish of curried chicken. 'Her cuisine is a little limited, but she has as good an idea of breakfast as a Scotswoman. What have you there, Watson?'

'Ham and eggs,' I answered.

Mrs. Hudson was a long-suffering woman. Not only was her first-floor flat invaded at all hours by throngs of singular and often undesirable characters, but her remarkable lodger showed an eccentricity and irregularity in his life which must have sorely tried her patience. His incredible untidiness, his addiction to music at strange hours, his occasional revolver practice within doors, his weird and often malodorous scientific experiments, and the atmosphere of violence and danger which hung around him made him the very worst tenant in London. On the other hand, his payments were princely. I have no doubt that the house might have been purchased at the price which Holmes paid for the rooms during the years I was with him. The landlady stood in the deepest awe of him, and never dared to interfere with him, however outrageous his proceedings might seem.* She was fond of him, too, for he had a remarkable gentleness and courtesy in his dealings with women. He disliked and distrusted the sex, but he was a chivalrous opponent.

* * * *

Holmes observed children with the same detachment as he brought to women. 'My dear Watson,' he once said to me; 'you as a medical man are continually gaining light as to the tendencies of a child by the study of the parents.

* There is a rumour that Mrs. Hudson left the manuscript of a short book entitled *My Illustrious Lodger*. This fascinating study of Holmes through the eyes of his landlady has never come to light. But the search continues – along with the search for the mathematical theses of Moriarty and the monographs of Holmes himself – EDITOR.

Bell Street, N. W. 1, 1904
(*City of Westminster Libraries, Archives Department*)

Don't you see that the converse is equally valid. I have frequently gained my first real insight into the character of parents by studying their children.'

I was not sure whether it was irony that made him exclaim, 'The Board Schools are lighthouses, my boy! Beacons of the future! Capsules, with hundreds of bright little seeds in each, out of which will spring the wiser, better England of the future.'

In more serious mood he said, 'Education never ends, Watson. It is a series of lessons, with the greatest for the last.'

*   *   *   *

There was never a more conscientious man at his job than Holmes.

'They say that genius is an infinite capacity for taking pains,' he remarked with a smile. 'It's a very bad definition, but it does apply to detective work.' But how often his patient work was ignored. 'Out of my last fifty-three cases my name has only appeared in four, and the police have had all credit in forty-nine.'

*   *   *   *

The agony columns of newspapers fascinated my friend. I remember him taking down the great book in which, day by day, he filed the agony columns of the various London journals. 'Dear me!,' said he, turning over the pages, 'what a chorus of groans, cries, and bleatings! What a rag-bag of singular happenings! But surely the most valuable hunting-ground that ever was given to a student of the unusual! This person is alone, and cannot be approached by letter without a breach of the absolute secrecy that is desired. How is any news or any message to reach him from without? Obviously by advertisement through a newspaper. There seems no other way, and fortunately we need concern ourselves with the one paper only. Here are the *Daily Gazette* extracts of the last fortnight. "Lady with a black boa at Prince's Skating Club" – that we may pass. "Surely Jimmy will not break his mother's heart" – that appears to be irrelevant. "If the lady who fainted in the Brixton bus" – she does not interest me. "Every day my heart longs —" Bleat, Watson – unmitigated bleat!'

*   *   *   *

Holmes's understanding of human nature came from his power of identification. 'You know my methods, Watson: I put myself in the man's place, and having first gauged his intelligence, I try to imagine how I should myself have proceeded under the same circumstances. But,' he added, 'it is of the first importance not to allow your judgement to be biased by personal qualities. A client is to me a mere unit, a factor in a problem. The emotional qualities are antagonistic to clear reasoning. I assure you that the most winning woman I ever knew was hanged for poisoning three little children for their insurance money, and the most repellant man of my acquaintance is a philanthropist who has spent nearly a quarter of a million upon the London poor.'

'These are surely exceptions.'

'I never make exceptions. An exception disproves the rule. Have you ever had occasion to study character in handwriting? What do you make of this fellow's scribble?'

'It is legible and regular,' I answered. 'A man of business habits and some force of character.'

Holmes shook his head.

'Look at his long letters,' he said. 'They hardly rise above the common herd. That *d* might be an *a*, and that *l* an *e*. Men of character always differentiate their long letters, however illegible they write. There is vacillation in his *k*'s and self-esteem in his capitals. I am going out now. I have some few references to make. Let me recommend this book – one of the most remarkable ever penned. It is Winwood Reade's *Martyrdom of Man*. I shall be back in an hour.'

I sat in the window with the volume in my hand, but my thoughts were far from the daring speculations of the writer. My mind ran upon a recent client, a Miss Mary Morstan – her smiles, the deep rich tones of her voice, the strange mystery which overhung her life. So I sat and mused, until such dangerous thoughts came into my head that I hurried away to my desk and plunged furiously into the latest treatise upon pathology.

HOLMES AND MYSELF

It was a cold morning of the early spring, and we sat after breakfast on either side of a cheery fire in our room in Baker Street. A thick fog rolled down between the lines of dun-coloured houses, and the opposing windows loomed like dark, shapeless blurs, through the heavy yellow wreaths. Our gas was lit, and shone on the white cloth, and glimmer of china and metal, for the table had not been cleared yet. Sherlock Holmes had been silent all the morning, dipping continuously into the advertisement columns of a succession of papers, until at last, having apparently given up his search, he had emerged in no very sweet temper to lecture me upon my literary short-comings.

'I glanced over your "Study in Scarlet",' said he. 'Honestly, I cannot congratulate you upon it. Detection is, or ought to be, an exact science, and should be treated in the same cold and unemotional manner. You have attempted to tinge it with romanticism, which produces much the same effect as if you worked a love-story or an elopement into the fifth proposition of Euclid.'

'But the romance was there,' I remonstrated. 'I could not tamper with the facts.'

'Some facts should be suppressed, or, at least, a just sense of proportion should be observed in treating them. The only point in the case which deserved mention was the curious analytical reasoning from effects to causes by which I succeeded in unravelling it.'

I was annoyed at this criticism of a work which had been specially designed to please him. I confess, too, that I was irritated by the egotism which seemed to demand that every line of my pamphlet should be devoted to his own special doings. I made no remark, however, but sat nursing my wounded leg. I had had a Jezail bullet through it, and though it did not prevent me from walking, it ached wearily at every change of the weather.

* * * *

'I must admit, Watson,' said Holmes on another occasion, 'that you have some power of selection which atones for much which I deplore in your narratives. Your fatal habit of looking at everything from the point of view of a story instead of as a scientific exercise has ruined what might have been an instructive and even classical series of demonstrations. You slur over work of the utmost finesse and delicacy in order to dwell upon sensational details which may excite but cannot possibly instruct the reader.'

'Why do you not write them yourself?' I said, with some bitterness.

'I will, my dear Watson, I will.'

* * * *

I did, however, get the occasional word of praise. 'It is pleasant to me to observe, Watson, that you have so far grasped this truth that in these little records of our cases which you have been good enough to draw up, and, I am bound to say, occasionally to embellish, you have given prominence not so much to the many *causes célèbres* and sensational trials in which I have figured, but rather to those incidents which may have been trivial in themselves, but which have given room for those faculties of deduction and of logical synthesis which I have made my special province.'

'And yet,' I said smiling, 'I cannot quite hold myself absolved from the charge of sensationalism which has been urged against my records.'

'You have erred, perhaps,' he observed, taking up a glowing cinder with the tongs, and lighting with it the long cherrywood pipe which was wont to replace his clay when he was in a disputatious rather than a meditative mood – 'you have erred, perhaps, in attempting to put colour and life into each of your statements,* instead of confining yourself to the task of placing upon record that severe reasoning from cause to effect which is really the only notable feature about the thing. Crime is common. Logic is rare. Therefore it is upon logic rather than upon crime that you should dwell.

'At the same time,' he remarked after a pause, during which he had sat puffing at his long pipe and gazing down into the fire, 'you can hardly be open to the charge of sensationalism, for out of these cases which you have been so kind as to interest yourself in, a fair proportion do not treat of crime in its legal sense at all. The small matter in which I endeavoured to help the King of Bohemia, the

* It has been suggested that Watson provided only the notes of the cases, and that they were put into narrative form by a writer named Conan Doyle – EDITOR.

singular experience of Miss Mary Sutherland, the problem connected with the man with the twisted lip and the incident of the noble bachelor, were all matters which are outside the pale of the law. But in avoiding the sensational I fear that you may have bordered on the trivial.'

'The end may have been so,' I answered, 'but the methods I hold to have been novel and of interest.'

'Pshaw, my dear fellow, what do the public, the great unobservant public, who could hardly tell a weaver by his tooth or a compositor by his left thumb, care about the finer shades of analysis and deduction! But, indeed, if you are trivial, I cannot blame you, for the days of the great cases are past. Man, or at least criminal man, has lost all enterprise and originality. As to my own little practice, it seems to be degenerating into an agency for recovering lost lead pencils and giving advice to young ladies from boarding-schools. I think that I have touched bottom at last.'

This remark was the prelude to one of our most famous cases, 'The Copper Beeches'!

*   *   *   *

Holmes loved to lie in the very centre of five millions of people, with his filaments stretching out and running through them, responsive to every little rumour or suspicion of unsolved crime. Finding that he was too absorbed for conversation I had tossed aside the barren paper and, leaning back in my chair, I fell into a brown study. Suddenly my companion's voice broke in upon my thoughts.

'You are right, Watson,' said he. 'It does seem a most preposterous way of settling a dispute.'

'Most preposterous!' I exclaimed, and then suddenly realizing how he had echoed the inmost thought of my soul, I sat up in my chair and stared at him in blank amazement.

'What is this, Holmes?' I cried. 'This is beyond anything which I could have imagined.'

He laughed heartily at my perplexity.

'You remember,' said he, 'that some little time ago when I read you the passage in one of Poe's sketches in which a close reasoner follows the unspoken thoughts of his companion, you were inclined to treat the matter as a mere *tour-de-force* of the author. On my remarking that I was constantly in the habit of doing the same thing you expressed incredulity.'

'Oh, no!'

'Perhaps not with your tongue, my dear Watson, but certainly with your eyebrows. So when I saw you throw down your paper and enter upon a train of thought, I was very happy to have the opportunity of reading it off, and eventually of breaking into it, as a proof that I had been *en rapport* with you.'

But I was still far from satisfied. 'In the example which you read to me,' said I, 'the reasoner drew his conclusions from the actions of the man whom he observed. If I remember right, he stumbled over a heap of stones, looked up at the stars, and so on. But I have been seated quietly in my chair, and what clues can I have given you?'

'You do yourself an injustice. The features are given to

man as the means by which he shall express his emotions, and yours are faithful servants.'

'Do you mean to say that you read my train of thoughts from my features?'

'Your features, and especially your eyes. Perhaps you cannot yourself recall how your reverie commenced?'

'No, I cannot.'

'Then I will tell you. After throwing down your paper, which was the action which drew my attention to you, you sat for half a minute with a vacant expression. Then your eyes fixed themselves upon your newly framed picture of General Gordon, and I saw by the alteration in your face that a train of thought had been started. But it did not lead very far. Your eyes flashed across to the unframed portrait of Henry Ward Beecher which stands upon the top of your books. Then you glanced up at the wall, and of course your meaning was obvious. You were thinking that if the portrait were framed, it would just cover that bare space and correspond with Gordon's picture over there.'

'You have followed me wonderfully!' I exclaimed.

'So far I could hardly have gone astray. But now your thoughts went back to Beecher, and you looked hard across as if you were studying the character in his features. Then your eyes ceased to pucker, but you continued to look across, and your face was thoughtful. You were recalling the incidents of Beecher's career. I was well aware that you could not do this without thinking of the mission which he undertook on behalf of the North at the time of the Civil War, for I remember your expressing your passionate indignation at the way in which he was received by the more turbulent of our people. You felt so strongly about it, that I knew you could not think of Beecher without thinking of that also. When a moment later I saw your eyes wander away from the picture, I suspected that your mind had now turned to the Civil War, and when I observed that your lips set, your eyes sparkled, and your hands clenched, I was positive that you were indeed thinking of the gallantry which was shown by both sides in the desperate struggle. But then, again, your face grew sadder; you shook your head. You were dwelling upon the sadness and horror and useless waste of life. Your hand stole towards your old wound and a smile quivered on your lips, which showed me that the ridiculous side of this method of settling international questions had forced itself upon your mind. At this point I agreed with you that it was preposterous, and was glad to find that all my deductions had been correct.'

'Absolutely!' said I. 'And now that you have explained it, I confess that I am amazed as before.'

'It was very superficial, my dear Watson, I assure you. I should not have intruded it upon your attention had you not shown some incredulity the other day.'

*   *   *   *

Holmes's allusion to my old bullet wound reminded me of his remarkable deduction that I had been in Afghanistan when we first met. 'You appeared to be surprised when I told you, on our first meeting, that you had come from Afghanistan. I *knew* you came from Afghanistan.

'From long habit the train of thoughts ran so swiftly through my mind that I arrived at the conclusion without being conscious of intermediate steps. There were such steps, however. The train of reasoning ran, "Here is a gentleman of the medical type, but with the air of a military man. Clearly an army doctor, then. He has just come from the tropics, for his face is dark, and that it is not the natural tint of the skin, for his wrists are fair. He has undergone hardship and sickness, as his haggard face says clearly. His left arm has been injured. He holds it in a stiff and unnatural manner. Where in the tropics could an English army doctor have seen much hardship and got his arm wounded?* Clearly in Afghanistan." The whole train of thought did not occupy a second. I then remarked that you came from Afghanistan, and you were astonished.'

* * * *

'You have spoken of observation and deduction,' I said. 'But surely the one to some extent implies the other.'

'Why, hardly,' he answered, leaning back luxuriously in his arm-chair, and sending up thick blue wreaths from his pipe. 'For example, observation shows me that you have been to the Wigmore Street Post Office this morning, but deduction lets me know that when there you dispatched a telegram.'

'Right!' said I. 'Right on both points! But I confess that I don't see how you arrived at it. It was a sudden impulse on my part, and I have mentioned it to no one.'

---

* Did Watson have two wounds, one in the arm and one in the leg? Elsewhere he speaks of a shoulder wound – EDITOR.

'It is simplicity itself,' he remarked, chuckling at my surprise – 'so absurdly simple than an explanation is superfluous; and yet it may serve to define the limits of observation and deduction. Observation tells me that you have a little reddish mould adhering to your instep. Just opposite the Wigmore Street Office they have taken up the pavement and thrown up some earth, which lies in such a way that it is difficult to avoid treading in it in entering. The earth is of this peculiar reddish tint which is found, as far as I know, nowhere else in the neighbourhood. So much is observation. The rest is deduction.'

'How, then, did you deduce the telegram?'

'Why, of course I knew that you had not written a letter since I sat opposite to you all morning. I see also in your open desk there that you have a sheet of stamps and a thick bundle of postcards. What could you go into a post office for, then, but to send a wire? Eliminate all other factors, and the one which remains must be the truth.'

'In this case it certainly is so,' I replied, after a little thought. 'The thing, however, is, as you say, of the simplest. Would you think me impertinent if I were to put your theories to a more severe test?'

'On the contrary,' he answered; 'it would prevent me from taking a second dose of cocaine. I should be delighted to look into any problem which you might submit to me.'

'I have heard you say that it is difficult for a man to have any object in daily use without leaving the impress of his individuality upon it in such a way that a trained observer might read it. Now, I have here a watch which has recently come into my possession. Would you have the kindness to let me have an opinion upon the character or habits of the late owner?'

I handed him over the watch with some slight feeling of amusement in my heart, for the test was, as I thought, an impossible one, and I intended it as a lesson against the somewhat dogmatic tone which he occasionally assumed. He balanced the watch in his hand, gazed hard at the dial, opened the back, and examined the works, first with his naked eyes and then with a powerful convex lens. I could hardly keep from smiling at his crestfallen face when he finally snapped the case to and handed it back.

'There are hardly any data,' he remarked. 'The watch has been recently cleaned, which robs me of my most suggestive facts.'

'You are right,' I answered. 'It was cleaned before being sent to me.'

In my heart I accused my companion of putting forward a most lame and impotent excuse to cover his failure. What data could he expect from an uncleaned watch?

'Though unsatisfactory, my research has not been entirely barren,' he observed, staring up at the ceiling with dreamy, lack-lustre eyes. 'Subject to your correction, I should judge that the watch belonged to your elder brother, who inherited it from your father.'

'That you gather, no doubt, from the H.W. upon the back?'

'Quite so. The W. suggests your own name. The date of the watch is nearly fifty years back and the initials are as old as the watch; so it was made for the last generation. Jewellery usually descends to the eldest son, and he is most likely to have the same name as the father. Your father has, if I remember right, been dead many years. It has, therefore, been in the hands of your eldest brother.'

'Right, so far,' said I. 'Anything else?'

'He was a man of untidy habits – very untidy and care-less. He was left with good prospects, but he threw away his chances, lived for some time in poverty with occasional short intervals of prosperity, and, finally, taking to drink, he died. That is all I can gather.'

I sprang from my chair and limped impatiently about the room with considerable bitterness in my heart.

'This is unworthy of you, Holmes,' I said. 'I could not have believed that you would have descended to this. You have made inquiries into the history of my unhappy brother, and you now pretend to deduce this knowledge in some fanciful way. You cannot expect me to believe that you have read all this from his old watch! It is unkind, and, to speak plainly, has a touch of charlatanism in it.'

'My dear Doctor,' said he, kindly, 'pray accept my apologies. Viewing the matter as an abstract problem, I had forgotten how personal and painful a thing it might be to you. I assure you, however, that I never even knew that you had a brother until you handed me the watch.'

'Then how in the name of all that is wonderful did you get these facts? They are absolutely correct in every particular.'

'Ah, that is good luck. I could only say what was the balance of probability. I did not at all expect to be accurate.'

'But it was not mere guesswork?'

'No, no: I began by stating that your brother was careless. When you observe the lower part of that catch-case you notice that it is not only dinted in two places, but it is cut and marked all over from the habit of keeping other hard objects, such as coins or keys, in the same pocket. Surely it is no great feat to assume that a man who treats a fifty-guinea watch so cavalierly must be a careless man. Neither is it a very far-fetched inference that a man who inherits one article of such value is pretty well provided for in other respects.'

I nodded to show that I followed his reasoning.

'It is very customary for pawnbrokers in England, when they take a watch, to scratch the number of the ticket with a pin-point upon the inside of the case. It is more handy than a label, as there is no risk of the number being lost or transposed. There are no less than four such numbers visible to my lens on the inside of this case. Inference – that your brother was often at low water. Secondary inference – that he had occasional bursts of prosperity, or he could not have redeemed the pledge. Finally, I ask you to look at the inner plate, which contains the keyhole. Look at the thousands of scratches all round the hole – marks where the key has slipped. What sober man's key could have scored those grooves? But you will never see a drunkard's watch without them. He winds it at night, and he leaves these traces of his unsteady hand. Where is the mystery in all this?'

'It is as clear as daylight,' I answered. 'I regret the injustice which I did you. I should have had more faith in your marvellous faculty. May I ask whether you have any professional inquiry on foot at present?'

'None. Hence the cocaine. I cannot live without brain-work. What else is there to live for? Stand at the window here. Was ever such a dreary, dismal, unprofitable world? See how the yellow fog swirls down the street and drifts across the dun-coloured houses. What could be more hopelessly prosaic and material? What is the use of having powers, doctor, when one has no field upon which to exert them? Crime is commonplace, existence is commonplace, and no qualities save those which are commonplace have any function upon earth.'

*   *   *   *

I cannot recall the many times in which I was Holmes's guinea-pig, but certain instructive and amusing examples come to my mind – as when I entered our room one evening and he said to me:

'You have been at your club all day, I perceive.'

'My dear Holmes!'

'Am I right?'

'Certainly, but how —?'

He laughed at my bewildered expression.

'There is a delightful freshness about you, Watson, which makes it a pleasure to exercise any small powers which I possess at your expense. A gentleman goes forth on a showery and miry day. He returns immaculate in the evening with a gloss still on his hat and boots. He has been a fixture, therefore, all day. He is not a man with intimate friends. Where, then, could he have been? Is it not obvious?'

'Well, it is rather obvious.'

'The world is full of obvious things which nobody by any chance ever observes.'

I well remember Holmes telling me how he could have deduced that my bedroom window was on the right side. 'I know the military neatness which characterizes you. You shave every morning, and in this season you shave by the sunlight, but since your shaving is less and less complete as we get farther back on the left side, until it becomes positively slovenly as we get round the angle of the jaw, it is surely very clear that that side is less well illuminated than the other. I could not imagine a man of your habits looking at himself in an equal light, and being satisfied with such a result. I only quote this as a trivial example of observation and inference.'

On another occasion he divined from my slippers that I had been unwell. I glanced down at the new patent leathers which I was wearing. 'How on earth —?' I began, but Holmes answered my question before it was asked.

'Your slippers are new,' he said. 'You could not have had them more than a few weeks. The soles which you are at this moment presenting to me are slightly scorched. For a moment I thought they might have got wet and been burned in the drying. But near the instep there is a small circular wafer of paper with the shopman's hieroglyphics upon it. Damp would of course have removed this. You had then been sitting with your feet outstretched to the fire, which a man would hardly do even in so wet a June as this if he were in his full health.'

Like all Holmes's reasoning, the thing seemed simplicity itself when it was once explained. He read the thought upon my features, and his smile had a tinge of bitterness.

'I am afraid that I rather give myself away when I

explain,' said he. 'Results without causes are much more impressive.'

My health was fairly good, but I was a believer in the Turkish Bath. 'But why Turkish?' asked my friend one day, gazing fixedly at my boots. I was reclining in a cane-backed chair at the moment, and my protruded feet had attracted his ever-active attention.

'English,' I answered, in some surprise. 'I got them at Latimer's, in Oxford Street.'

Holmes smiled with an expression of weary patience.

'The bath!' he said, 'the bath! Why the relaxing and expensive Turkish rather than the invigorating home-made article?'

'Because for the last few days I have been feeling rheumatic and old. A Turkish bath is what we call an alterative in medicine – a fresh starting-point, a cleanser of the system.

'By the way, Holmes,' I added. 'I have no doubt the connection between my boots and a Turkish bath is a perfectly self-evident one to a logical mind, and yet I should be obliged to you if you would indicate it.'

'The train of reasoning is not very obscure, Watson,' said Holmes, with a mischievous twinkle. 'It belongs to the same elementary class of deduction which I should illustrate if I were to ask you who shared your cab in your drive this morning.'

'I don't admit that a fresh illustration is an explanation,' said I, with some asperity.

'Bravo, Watson! A very dignified and logical remonstrance. Let me see, what were the points? Take the last one first – the cab. You observe that you have some splashes on the left sleeve and shoulder of your coat. Had you sat in the centre of a hansom you would probably have had no splashes, and if you had they would certainly have been symmetrical. Therefore it is clear that you sat at the side. Therefore it is equally clear that you had a companion.'

'That is very evident.'

'Absurdly commonplace, is it not?'

'But the boots and the bath?'

'Equally childish. You are in the habit of doing up your boots in a certain way. I see them on this occasion fastened with an elaborate double bow, which is not your usual method of tying them. You have, therefore, had them off. Who has tied them? A bootmaker – or the boy at the bath. It is unlikely that it is the bootmaker, since your boots are nearly new. Well, what remains. The bath. Absurd, is it not? You do not observe, Watson. For example you have frequently seen the steps that which lead up from the hall to this room.'

'Frequently.'

'How often?'

'Well, some hundreds of times.'

'Then how many are there?'

'How many! I don't know.'

'Quite so! You have not observed. And yet you have seen.* That is just my point. Now, I know that there are seventeen steps, because I have both seen and observed.'

*   *   *   *

* Holmes's distinction between seeing and observing in the physical field has an interesting parallel in F. C. Copleston's theory of seeing and noticing in the intellectual field. Copleston, in *Contemporary Philosophy* (Ch. VI), argues that we often go wrong in our reasoning because we fail to notice what is relevant – EDITOR.

'So, Watson,' said Holmes suddenly, 'you do not propose to invest in South African securities?'

I gave a start of astonishment. Accustomed as I was to Holmes's curious faculties, this sudden intrusion into my most intimate thoughts was utterly inexplicable.

'How on earth do you know that?' I asked.

He wheeled round upon his stool, with a steaming test-tube in his hand and a gleam of amusement in his deep-set eyes.

'Now, Watson, confess yourself utterly taken aback,' said he.

'I am.'

'I ought to make you sign a paper to that effect.'

'Why?'

'Because in five minutes you will say that it is all so absurdly simple.'

'I am sure that I shall say nothing of the kind.'

'You see, my dear Watson' – he propped his test-tube in the rack and began to lecture with an air of a professor addressing his class – 'it is not really difficult to construct a series of inferences, each dependent upon its predecessor and each simple in itself. If, after doing so, one simply knocks out all the central inferences and presents one's audience with the starting-point and the conclusion, one may produce a startling, though possibly a meretricious, effect. Now, it was not really difficult, by an inspection of the groove between your left forefinger and thumb, to feel sure that you did *not* propose to invest your small capital in the gold-fields.'

'I see no connection.'

'Very likely not; but I can quickly show you a close

connection. Here are the missing links of the very simple chain: 1. You had chalk between your left finger and thumb when you returned from the club last night. 2. You put chalk there when you play billiards to steady the cue. 3. You never play billiards except with Thurston. 4. You told me four weeks ago that Thurston had an option on some South African property which would expire in a month, and which he desired you to share with him. 5. Your cheque-book is locked in my drawer, and you have not asked for the key. 6. You do not propose to invest your money in this manner.'

'How absurdly simple,' I cried.

'Quite so!' said he, a little nettled. 'Every problem becomes very childish when once it is explained to you.'

*　　*　　*　　*

The relations between Holmes and myself were peculiar. He was a man of habits, narrow and concentrated habits, and I had become one of them. As an institution I was like the violin, the shag tobacco, the old black pipe, the index books, and others perhaps less excusable. When it was a case of active work and a comrade was needed upon whose nerve he could place some reliance, my role was obvious. But apart from this I had uses. I was a whetstone for his mind. I stimulated him. He liked to think aloud in my presence. His remarks could hardly be said to be made to me – many of them would have been as appropriately addressed to his bedstead – but none the less, having formed the habit, it had become in some way helpful that I should register and interject. If I irritated him by a certain methodical slowness in my mentality, that irritation served only to make his own flame-like intuitions and impressions flash up the more vividly and swiftly. Such was my humble role in our alliance.

Sometimes, I think, he realized that I had been of use to him in a small way. 'You have a grand gift of silence, Watson,' he once said. 'It makes you quite invaluable as a companion.' And I shall not easily forget his words to me the day before the great storm of 4 August 1914 swept over Europe.

'Good old Watson! You are the one fixed point in a changing age.'

Melcombe Street, N. W. 1, 1898

(City of Westminster Libraries, Archives Department)

EPILOGUE

It was late in the evening. Holmes lay with his gaunt figure stretched in his deep chair, his pipe curling forth slow wreaths of acrid tobacco, while his eyelids drooped over his eyes so lazily that he might almost have been asleep.

'What is the meaning of life, Watson?' he said. 'What object is served by this circle of misery and violence and fear? It must tend to some end, or else our universe is ruled by chance, which is unthinkable. But what end? There is the great standing perennial problem to which human reason is as far as ever. We reach. We grasp. And what is left in our hands at the end? A shadow. Our highest assurance of the goodness of Providence seems to me to rest in the flowers. All other things, our powers, our desires, our food, are really necessary for our existence in the first instance. But the rose is an extra. Its smell and its colour are an embellishment of life, not a condition of it. It is only goodness which gives extras, and so I say again that we have much to hope from the flowers.'

He took up his violin from the corner, and began to play some low, dreamy, melodious air – his own, no doubt, for he had a remarkable gift for improvisation. Then I seemed to be floated peacefully away upon a soft sea of sound. . . .

INDEX

INDEX

Watson, Dr. John H.: Bohemianism,
    18
  club man, 94
  dislike of rows, 11
  father and brother, 91–93
  gift for silence, 100
  military neatness, 95
  one of Holmes' habits, 99

smoking 'Ships' tobacco, 11
steadfastness, 100
'Stormy Petrel of Crime', 25
narratives criticized by Holmes,
    82–85,
Wigmore Street Post Office, 89, 90
Wodehouse, P. G., 69,
Women, 76–78